GHOSTRIDERS II

Taking the Night By Storm...

MICHAEL TORRENCE

Published by Michael Torrence

Book Design by
DreamEmpire Publishing

Edited by
Joyce Licorish

Cover Art by
Joyce Licorish & Miki Morrow

Printed in the United States of America
First Printing Edition, Fall 2024

Copy written with the Library of Congress

Some names and identifying details of people in this book have been altered to protect their privacy.

ISBN: 979-8-9904266-2-7

CONTENTS

ACKNOWLEDGEMENTS

First, I give my thanks to Jehovah God for every positive thing in my life. Through Him, all things are possible. To my sis and my sponsor, always by my side—thank you for your endless support. My parents, and especially Ms. Lady, thank you. Rest in peace, Cotton Top. I love you. To my children, John and Tiffany, and all my grandchildren—I love you all deeply.

Special thanks to Jessica Garza for the time and effort you put into editing and typing this book. Thank you, Donna Bevers, for everything you've done and all the support you've given me. Mr. House, much appreciation! To Renee, Michelle, Shoun, Teresa, and Charles Jr., I love you all. Uncle James Jones, thank you. Deadra Dorsey, my thanks to you too. May Jehovah bless us all.

A big thanks to Dream Empire for the cover and all the extra hands on deck to bring this book to life. And to all my supporters—thank you for riding with me!

CHAPTER ONE

Weed got up around 5 a.m. He couldn't really sleep. Looking out the kitchen window, he saw it was foggy outside. He opened the back door to check the temperature—felt pretty good for a June morning. It was June 2, 2025. His birthday. It was also the day the crew chose to split the pot from the take they got off Snake and Jesse. Weed hadn't seen Terry, Lil Bitt, or Red since they all went their separate ways in Florida after Moto Weekend. He wasn't sure if Red would show; they left on good terms but on a neutral slate.

He'd been riding with Doc whenever he could. They hadn't missed a bike meet yet, down to ride anywhere, anytime. Weed still had both his bikes—the 850 Suzuki and the KZ11000. And Sexy was still by his side, holding strong. Weed and Ms. D were married now, too. His phone started ringing, and he was pretty sure it was her. She was always up and at work early.

"Hello?"

"Happy birthday, baby!"

"Thank you, sweetheart."

"Why you up so early?"

“Couldn’t sleep, baby. Got a lot on my mind and plenty to handle today.”

“Oh, yeah, you did tell me you gotta meet with Doc early.”

“Yeah, I’ll call him in an hour or so, see if he’s up.”

“Alright, baby. Gotta get back to work. Just wanted to be the first to say happy birthday.”

“Thanks, love. I appreciate it. I love you.”

“Love you too.”

Ms. D hung up, and Weed saw he had three new texts. The first one was from Crystal. He hadn’t seen her since he dropped her off in Fort Wayne. He’d set her up in an apartment there, even covered her rent for the first year. Her text read, “Hope to see you today. It’s your birthday, and I got something for you.” He replied that he’d see her, though he wasn’t sure on the time yet. He’d hit her up as soon as he talked to Doc.

Next message was from Terry and Lil Bitt, both wishing him a happy soul day and saying they hoped to see him later. He thanked them and said they’d definitely link up, just didn’t have a set time yet.

The last text was from his sister Tiffany. “Happy birthday, bro. I’ll be in Naptown tomorrow to see you.” He hit her back, “Ok sis. Love you!”

Figuring it was time to get moving, Weed jumped in the shower. Not even a minute in, his phone started ringing again. He reached out, checked the caller ID, saw it was Sexy, and picked up.

“Weed, happy birthday, baby!”

"Thank you, Sexy. How you doin'?"

"I'm good. Just leaving the club." Sexy was still president of the Ghost Riders, and the two of them were tight. "So, what's up with you this morning?"

"Waiting to hear from Doc, see what's good for today."

"Weed, am I gonna see you today, or is it like last year—running off with your wife?"

"Not sure if she's got plans, but we'll get together at some point."

"Alright, just checking. By the way, I got another one of those calls yesterday from Snake's old club, threatening my life."

"I told you, Sexy, we'd handle it if they called again. Now that they have, we're on it. Text me the number, I'll get it traced."

"I'm on it, Weed."

"Cool. I'll call you back soon."

Weed hung up with Sexy and finished his shower. After dressing, he called Doc.

"What's up, Doc?"

"Happy soul day, Tumbleweed."

"Thanks, man. How you doin'?"

"I'm good, just looking after Pam. She's coming down with a cold, not feeling well."

"Sorry to hear that. Tell her I hope she feels better."

“Will do. I know you’re wondering about today’s plan.”

“Yeah, I am.”

“Well, we can meet anytime, but I gotta be straight with you. Finding a good buyer hasn’t been easy.”

“Got it. That’s on me for trying to unload it all at once. We might have to talk to Crystal, see what she remembers about where it all came from, then move it bit by bit.”

“Sounds good to me.”

“Also, we gotta act on that problem with Snake’s old club. Sexy got another call last night.”

“Count me in, partner.”

“Alright. Let’s say we meet at a hotel by the airport around 3 p.m.”

“Sounds like a plan.”

In Indianapolis, folks knew who was local and who wasn’t. Weed didn’t want to draw attention. He texted everyone with the time and place, saying he’d send the room number once they arrived. Then he called a friend to trace the number that had been threatening Sexy. He’d gotten tight with a lady named Donna, who worked as a probation officer and had some useful connections. She was a beauty—4'11", caramel skin, thick in all the right places. She picked up on the third ring.

“Hello, Weed. How you doin’?”

“I’m good, Donna.”

“So, what brings you to callin’ me?”

“I need a favor. I have a number I need traced—name, address, if possible?”

“Text me the number, and give me twenty minutes. I don’t want to hold onto the info too long, alright?”

“Got it. Number is 213-562-5327. Thanks, Donna.”

Weed hung up and called Sexy, asking if she wanted to grab some breakfast. She was down, so he went to the garage, fired up the 850—it was as loud as ever. Letting it warm up, he threw on his jacket and helmet, locked up, grabbed the garage remote, and rolled out to meet Sexy on 86th and Ditch for breakfast.

CHAPTER TWO

By the time Weed met up with Sexy at the Ma and Pa restaurant, he was already five minutes late calling Donna back. He hurried over to park next to her bike and dialed Donna's number. She picked up on the second ring.

"Hold on a minute, Weed. Got someone in the office with me." He motioned for Sexy to stay quiet, and she nodded. After a moment, Donna came back on the line. "Weed, I told you twenty minutes."

"I know, I'm sorry. I'll make it up to you tomorrow, I promise."

"Alright, the number belongs to Frank Day. He's out of Oakland, but the number traces to L.A. He's got a long rap sheet and rides with an MC out of Los Angeles."

"Got it. Can you text me the address, Donna?"

"Sure thing, Weed."

"Thanks, Donna. I'll call you first thing in the morning."

"And happy birthday, Weed."

"Thanks, Donna, but I didn't tell you it was my birthday."

“I ran your name after we met,” she said with a laugh.

Weed chuckled. “Okay, Donna. Am I clear to hang with?”

“I guess so, Weed.”

“Alright, gotta go. Later, Donna.”

“Bye, Weed.”

Weed hung up, and he and Sexy headed into the restaurant. They sat down, but he could see she was deep in thought. He, too, was already thinking about his next move on this Frank Day character in L.A. After they ordered, he turned to her.

“What’s on your mind, Sexy?”

“Weed, I’ve got a lot going on. I can’t afford to just up and head to Cali to track down this dude!”

“Sexy, I owe you for what went down in Cali and Florida. I don’t need you to go out there—I’ll take care of it, promise.”

She just smiled, reassured. They ordered breakfast and started talking over plans for later in the day, as well as some help they might need moving the jewelry they’d gotten. Mid-meal, Weed’s phone buzzed. It was Jessie’s sister.

“Happy birthday, Tumbleweed.”

“Thank you,” he replied, glancing at Sexy to make sure she stayed quiet. “How you been?”

She said she was fine, keeping it short. Then she added, “There’s something you can help me with—two women who robbed my brother.”

He tried to play it off. "Not sure how I could help you with that."

She said Lil Bitt had mentioned maybe knowing him, but Weed denied knowing anyone by that name.

"Alright, thanks for your time on your birthday. Enjoy it," she replied.

"Thanks, I'll try." He hung up, suddenly losing his appetite. How could she connect him to Lil Bitt? Before he could think it through, another call came in—from Terry, who didn't sound good. She admitted she'd been getting threatening calls for years, but only now did they call her by her old nickname, Lil Bitt. He asked her to send him the number and assured her he'd take care of it. She agreed and hung up. Weed started feeling like his birthday was going south. The L.A. Deuces were turning into a major problem.

Then a text from Donna popped up: "Frank Day, a.k.a. Savage." She added that he was with the L.A. Deuces. He made a mental note, thanked her, and sent her the number Terry gave him, asking her to trace it.

Weed thought about calling in some backup. Over the past few years, he'd gotten close with Flaco, his sister's ex-boyfriend from California. Flaco was Mexican and rode like nobody Weed had ever seen. He had his own crew and, like Weed and Doc, they were independent—no colors. Weed shot Flaco a text, asking if he could call in an hour to discuss business. Flaco agreed, and Weed thanked him.

Soon after, Donna called him back, asking if everything was okay. Weed paused, figuring he might need her help down the line, so he kept it cool. "Yeah, everything's fine. Thanks, Donna."

"Alright, Weed. Just let me know if you need anything."

"Thanks," he replied, hanging up. He looked over at Sexy, who just shook her head. He reached across the table, put his hand over hers, and told her, "Everything will be alright." He flagged down the waitress for the check.

Sexy leaned in. "I think you're gonna need help from some patch holders."

"You having second thoughts?" he asked.

"Yeah," she replied. She knew if they were dealing with club colors, she should be involved. Weed told her he'd catch up with her after he talked to Flaco and Doc to get a read on things. They walked out to their bikes, both wrapped up in their own thoughts. As he reached his bike, Weed's phone buzzed—a text from his sister, asking if he was okay. He just shook his head, shot back a quick reply, and then hugged Sexy before watching her pull off.

He hit the highway to Doc's with a lot on his mind. This birthday was turning into anything but a celeBrotion. He needed to think about his ask for Flaco and how to approach it. Trust was everything in this situation, and he suspected his sister's text might be Flaco's doing, her checking on him because Flaco mentioned he'd called.

Weed gunned his bike, letting loose on the highway to clear his head. As he approached Doc's exit, he slowed down, pulled into a gas station, and dialed Doc's number from a pay phone. Doc picked up on the second ring.

"I feel your pain, Weed," Doc said out of nowhere.

Weed just smiled, shaking his head. "I'm five minutes out, Doc."

"Come on over," Doc replied before hanging up.

CHAPTER THREE

Weed pulled up to Doc's and parked in the driveway. Once inside, he greeted Doc and Pam, then made his way to the kitchen table, dialing up Flaco with Doc sitting across from him. Flaco picked up on the first ring, and Weed put him on speaker.

"Flaco, how's everything out west?"

"It's cool for now. Why you asking like that, Weed?"

"You know anything about an MC called the L.A. Deuces?"

"Weed, I know every club in this city. What you need to know?"

"You know a guy named Savage in the Deuces?"

"Yeah, I do. Real name's Frank Day. He's Snake's son—the one who got killed a few years back, around Moto Weekend."

"How well you know him?"

"He's VP of the Deuces, and he's exactly what his name says—a savage. He's been on a hunt, looking for who took a load of cash and jewelry from his pops, plus who took him out. What else you need to know?"

"Is he one of your boys?"

"No, I can't stand him."

"Mind if I ask why?"

"It's personal."

"Alright. If I asked for your help against him, would you be down?"

"Whatever you need, Weed. I got you and your family."

"Appreciate that. First, I need an address on him. I'll be in Cali in two weeks. Can I count on you?"

"I'll have the address texted to you soon as I get it."

"Thanks, Flaco. I'll be waiting for that text." Weed hung up, looked over at Doc, who shook his head.

"We need to talk to the crew, Weed. It's time they know what's going on."

"I'm with you, Doc." They talked it over, then Weed called Crystal, waiting as the phone rang. She finally answered on the fourth ring.

"Weed, I'm getting ready now to head up to Nap."

"Good, I have a quick question though."

"What's that, Weed?"

"You remember anything about where Snake and Jesse got all this product from?"

"We'll talk when I get there, Weed, okay?"

"Alright, we're meeting at a hotel out by the airport. I'll send you the room number when you arrive."

"Sounds good."

Weed hung up, confirming the details with Doc, then asked how much cash and jewelry was on hand to split among everyone.

"Weed, I can tell you I have around 12 million here in cash. I've got only about a quarter of the jewelry, keeping the rest safe elsewhere."

"That's smart," Weed nodded. He told Doc to split the cash for now and let everyone know they'd get more once they found a buyer for the jewelry and covered what was needed for protection. Doc agreed, suggesting they give each person $1.25 million to keep extra on hand for travel, weapons, or help if they needed it. Weed agreed with Doc's plan and told him to pay everyone who was in Florida, including himself, Pam, and Doc.

Right then, Weed got a text from Ms. D saying she'd be home soon and wanted to see him. He grinned and told Doc he was headed home until the meet. As he walked out, he told Pam to get well, gave Doc a quick hug, then hopped on his bike. He wasn't sure what route to take, but with three hours until the meet, he hit the highway to spend as much time with Ms. D as he could. He rode hard, hitting home faster than ever, making it in just nine minutes. As he pulled into the driveway, the garage door was already open, and there stood his wife, wearing a new teddy he'd never seen before. Weed wasted no time, parking and moving toward her as she pressed the button to close the garage.

He hugged and kissed her, reaching for his phone to shut it off, but noticed a new text—from Flaco. He told Ms. D to give him a second, opened the message, and saw it was an address. He thanked Flaco, turned off his phone, and headed to the bedroom with his wife. They spent the whole three hours wrapped up in each other, savoring the time alone.

As time ticked down, Weed knew he had business to handle. He told his wife he'd shower and get ready for the meet with Doc. She suggested they shower together, so she could get prepped for work, and he smiled. "Alright, my queen," he said, heading to the shower with her. The water hit him, bringing him back to focus, but as soon as she joined him, he knew they wouldn't be in a rush. The shower went on longer than expected.

Finally dressed, Weed grabbed his phone and headed to the kitchen. He noticed a cake with "Happy Birthday James!" on it. Cutting himself a piece, he picked up his ringing phone—Doc on the caller ID.

"What's up, partner?"

"Where you at, Weed?"

"I'm home. What's going on?"

"We need to talk, now. We got two problems to handle."

"Alright. You at the hotel?"

"Yeah."

"Let me finish this birthday cake real quick, and I'm on my way. Won't take long—I'll be on two wheels."

"Bring your friend too."

"It's that serious?"

"Just in case."

"Got it. Later."

Weed hung up, quickly ate his cake, and went upstairs to the safe. He grabbed his .45, along with Ms. D's gun, then found her in the bedroom. Wrapping his arms around her waist, he kissed her on the neck. "I love you," he told her.

She turned, returning the kiss, and reminded him to be careful. "I love you, too."

Weed kissed her forehead, then headed out to the garage. He chose to ride Old School again—the 850. Checking the gas gauge, he saw he needed a fill-up, so he started up the bike, threw on his jacket and lid, and cut out of the garage, hitting the door button on his way out. Glancing back once to make sure it was closing, he gripped the throttle, feeling the bike surge under him. He stopped at the gas station up the street, filled up, and hit the highway, pushing the bike all the way to make up for lost time. Riding hard and fast, he had his friend by his side and his crew on his mind, hoping everything was good with them too. As his exit came into view, his mind flashed to what they might be facing again—the lives lost last time, the jewelry they were still holding. Things were about to get real serious.

CHAPTER FOUR

Weed pulled up to the hotel about twenty minutes later, spotting Doc sitting in his truck, looking out for him. Weed parked next to him, then climbed into the truck with Doc and Pam.

"Weed, Sexy was shot at on the highway on her way here. She's safe, though—she's at a burger joint her brother owns," Doc said.

Weed felt his phone viBroting earlier but hadn't been able to check it. As Doc spoke, he pulled out his phone and saw two missed calls from Sexy, along with a text: "You're probably with Doc by now and know what happened. I'm ok, just please call me!"

"Anything else I need to know, Doc?"

Doc nodded toward a car where Terry and Lil Bitt sat with a man Weed didn't recognize. "This is why I told you to bring your friend," Doc said.

"Got it," Weed replied.

"Terry texted me saying Lil Bitt wouldn't come without this guy, but she's not feeling him," Doc explained.

"Alright, let's get everyone out of the cars. I need a quick word with Lil Bitt," Weed said.

"Let's get this show on the road, then."

Weed got out of the truck and called Sexy. "Hello, Weed."

"You alright, Sexy?"

"Just a little shook up, that's all."

"Can you get someone to bring you out to the hotel?"

"I wanted to check with you first."

"It's cool. I'll be waiting for you in the parking lot."

"Okay, on my way."

He hung up and walked over to the car with Terry, Lil Bitt, and the stranger. He asked Lil Bitt to step out of the car. She smiled at him and asked, "Can my man come too?"

Weed looked the guy over, then turned to Lil Bitt. "No disrespect, but I need to talk to you alone."

Terry got out and pulled Weed aside, whispering that she didn't trust the guy and had just met him last week. Weed thanked her with a kiss on the cheek, and she walked over to Doc's truck. When Weed turned back, Lil Bitt was getting out, so he led her over to his bike to talk privately.

"Weed, slow down a minute and talk to me," Lil Bitt said.

"We're going to my bike."

"Can we talk there?"

"Yes."

From the corner of his eye, Weed saw Crystal approaching. He motioned for her to go to the truck with Terry and Doc, and she walked by without saying a word. Once alone, Weed turned back to Lil Bitt.

"So, why'd you bring him along?"

"He's my man, and he didn't trust me coming to meet you alone since I told him we used to be together."

"Look, Lil Bitt, it's fine to be honest, but if he doesn't trust you, you don't need him. Now, because he's here, things are all out of whack. Can you get rid of him long enough for us to handle business?"

"I'll try, but if not?"

"Then you both gotta go, and Terry will catch you up later."

"Okay, I'll talk to him and figure something out."

"Do what you gotta do, but hurry."

As Lil Bitt walked off, Weed called Doc to check if he'd booked a room here.

"No, partner. The room's at the next hotel up the street," Doc replied. "By the way, Sexy's on her way here. I'll see if she can ride with Crystal to the next spot."

"Thanks." Weed hung up, noticing that Lil Bitt and her guy were getting loud, attracting attention. He walked over to Terry and asked whose car it was.

"It's a rental under my name," she replied.

“Alright, come with me. Let’s put both of them out, and then you can follow Doc.”

“I can do that.”

As they approached, Weed’s phone buzzed, and just then, Lil Bitt’s man slapped her hard across the face. Instinct kicked in—Weed yanked open the door, grabbed the guy, and pulled him out. Before he knew it, Doc was beside him, landing punches of his own. It took Pam to pull Doc back, and then Sexy, Crystal, and Terry arrived, dragging Weed off the guy. They’d both gotten their licks in, though.

With a parking lot camera nearby, Weed told Sexy to ride with Crystal and asked Terry and Lil Bitt to follow Doc and Pam. He turned to the guy on the ground, who now just wanted to go home, and handed him fifty bucks.

“Here, wait inside for a ride,” Weed said.

They walked into the hotel lobby, where a white lady behind the desk looked over at them. “Can I help you?”

“My friend here needs a spot to wait for a ride.”

“That’s fine, as long as there’s no more fighting. I only didn’t call the police because I saw him hit that young lady who’s left.”

“Thanks. What would it take for that footage to stay off the record?”

“Nothing—just get him out of here soon.”

“Done.” Weed called one of his guys from the MC, who said he was on his way to pick up the guy. Weed figured the guy might’ve been good for Lil Bitt if he’d just kept his hands to himself and trusted her. But that was no longer his concern. Without even asking the guy's name, Weed went outside to wait, watching as his friend Free arrived. Weed watched them pull off before he jumped on his bike and rode to the next hotel.

He parked beside Crystal's car, then texted Doc, asking what room they were in. Doc replied quickly, saying he'd meet him in the lobby. When Weed arrived, an older Black man behind the desk was observing everything. Doc approached the man, spoke to him, and nodded for Weed to follow him.

In the elevator, Doc turned to him. "That's my cousin down there. He's watching the room and everyone coming in."

"Smart move," Weed replied.

"We need to head to room 213 and get the money first. I was waiting for you to handle this part, partner."

As the doors opened, Weed looked at Doc and grinned, shaking his head and thinking *great minds think alike.*

CHAPTER FIVE

The rest of the evening went smoothly until they hit the topic of needing backup in California to handle the situation there. Weed explained that the problem was now on their doorstep since someone had taken shots at Sexy on the highway while she was on her way to meet up with them. It seemed that Snake's son, Savage, had been digging for his dad's treasure, and all signs pointed to Sexy. Now, they needed to handle it.

Terry and Crystal were the first to raise their hands for the trip, followed by Pam, who said she was in if Doc was. Sexy was definitely going, and of course, Weed wasn't about to stay back. That left only Lil Bitt, but she stayed quiet.

Then came the moment everyone had been waiting for—the money. Doc passed around extra-large freezer bags, each containing $1.25 million. As soon as everyone took theirs, Doc was about to bring up the jewels when Weed got a text from Free: "It's done. Hit me if you need me, one!"

Weed turned his attention back to Doc, just as Crystal started talking, answering his earlier question about the jewels. "The A-rabs who own the jewels are from D.C. They got hit in Vegas when their transport team was moving them. They use a crew of young, business-type guys to run their money, jewelry, drugs, and even women. They used to rely on Jessie and his crew for protection."

"Alright, I've got a question," Weed cut in.

"Shoot," Crystal replied.

"How do we get them to buy back the jewels?"

"We need to track them down first, then find a way in."

"You know how we can do that, Crystal?"

"We'll need to go to Vegas."

"Alright, looks like we're headed to Vegas after Cali. Who's in for that trip too?" Weed asked.

Everyone raised their hand, including Lil Bitt. Weed took a long look around at his crew, realizing just how much they'd all changed since the last time they were together. Lil Bitt still had her sex appeal, but dark circles under her eyes and a little extra weight. Terry looked mostly the same, though her style was more mature now. Crystal, though—she'd lost that innocent look, now exuding a mature, confident vibe. Doc had streaks of gray along his hairline, and even Pam showed a few signs of age. Sexy, though, still had that same striking look, phat in all the right ways. Weed's phone buzzed, breaking him from his thoughts. It was Flaco.

"What's up, Flaco?" he answered.

"All good, for now. How are you, Weed?"

"I'm fine, just waiting to hear from my sister."

"Well, that's why I'm calling, Weed."

"Oh yeah?"

"Yeah, Savage has your sister. He's demanding the jewels in exchange for her."

"Hold up a sec." Weed put his phone on speaker. "Flaco, repeat that."

Flaco's voice filled the room. "Savage has your sister, Weed. Word on the street is he thinks she's Sexy's sister. Nobody knows about you—just Sexy and Crystal. He wants his dad's jewels back."

"Flaco, any idea where he's keeping her?"

"I've got a lead, but I'm not certain yet."

"Alright, work on that, and I'll call you back soon." Weed hung up, then called Ms. D. "Get me the next flight out from Indy to California," he said, and hung up.

Everyone in the room, including Lil Bitt, immediately started booking flights to California. Weed walked over to Crystal, who was already off her phone.

"What's up, Crystal?" he asked.

"Weed, I'm sorry about Tiffany, but we're going to fight like hell to get her back!"

"We sure are, Crystal."

"And when this is all over, I'd like a moment alone with you before you walk away from me again."

"No problem, Crystal, you know that."

Just then, her phone rang. "It's my babysitter. I need to take this," she said, stepping aside. Weed glanced at Doc, who motioned for him to follow into an adjoining room. Once they were alone, Doc turned to him.

"Weed, how well do you know Flaco?"

"He and my sister have been off and on for years. I've ridden with him and his crew each time I'm in Cali, so I know him decently."

"Alright, then we need to move fast, because none of us know Savage, except Flaco."

"I'm with you on that, Doc." Weed's phone buzzed. It was Ms. D.

"Baby?" she asked.

"Yeah?"

"Your flight leaves from Naptown in two hours—that's the best I could get. Now, can you tell me why I'm booking you a flight last minute?"

"Baby, my sister's been kidnapped by some fool out west, and I'm going to get her back."

"I know you will, Weed, and heaven help anyone who's harmed her."

"Yeah. Love you, baby. I'll be home soon to drop off a package before I go."

"I'll be waiting."

Weed hung up, and he and Doc walked back into the main room, where Sexy was finishing a call with one of her club brothers. She hung up and looked around, her gaze settling on Weed.

"What's going on?" he asked.

She took a deep breath. "Weed, it's true—Savage has your sister. He wants all the jewels and money his father lost. He also wants me to bring him Crystal, claiming it's her fault. He's giving me a week, or he'll kill your sister."

"Alright, we'll handle this. I'll meet everyone in Cali—unless you're on the same flight leaving in an hour and 45 minutes?"

Everyone raised their hand; they were all on the same flight.

"Alright, I'll see you all at the airport." He turned to Sexy. "Let's get you to your club so you can take care of your loose ends."

They all left the hotel together. Weed handed Sexy his helmet so she'd be unrecognizable, then got her to the clubhouse safely, giving her a hug before taking off for home. This time, he was pushing for a record, racing across town to make the short time he had. He took 465, the interstate that circled the city, and twenty minutes later, he pulled into his driveway. Ms. D was waiting in her BMW with the garage door open.

He parked, grabbed his bag and pistol, and jumped in her truck. She turned on the soft strains of Luther Vandross, holding his hand as he let thoughts of his sister fill his mind. Halfway there, she reached over, lacing her fingers with his as he tried to control the pain inside. His sister was everything to him, and someone was going to pay. He must have dozed off because the next thing he knew, she was gently kissing him awake.

"We're here," she said softly.

He stirred, reached for her, and kissed her before grabbing his phone to call Doc. He noticed missed calls from Sexy and Terry but dialed Doc first.

Doc picked up on the second ring. "What's up, partner?"

"I'm out front of the airport. Where you at?"

"Pam and I are in an Uber, just entering the airport loop. We'll be there in a minute. Have you talked to Sexy or Terry?"

"No, just saw their missed calls."

"Well, I see you in the truck. We're four cars back."

"Alright, I'm getting out." Weed reached for the door handle, then saw his wife doing the same. He stepped out, and she held him tightly, whispering for him to be careful and come back to her. He looked into her eyes. "I love you," he said. "I'll be careful."

As he pulled away, Doc arrived, joking, "Y'all need a room?" Ms. D hugged Pam, who had become close to her since the wedding, and they shared a few laughs before Doc's phone rang. Thinking it was Sexy, Doc handed it to Weed.

Weed answered with a simple "Hello," not seeing the caller ID. It was Terry.

"Weed? I'm on my way with Lil Bitt. Just wanted to let you know I got another call from Jessie's sister while I was on my way home."

"Alright, Terry. Anything I need to know now?"

"Well, she's threatening to kill me if I don't come up with her brother's money and jewels. And this time, she mentioned your name too."

"Alright, Terry. I get your concern. We'll talk as soon as you get here."

CHAPTER SIX

The flight to California felt longer than usual for some reason, but Weed made it through. The whole crew had made it, and now they were waiting for a ride from Flaco. Weed hadn't let him know they were on the way, so they'd have to wait a bit. Spotting a gift shop, Weed saw a single Black & Mild with a wood tip. He hadn't smoked one in over seven years, but he really needed it today. He bought it and stepped back outside, asking Lil Bitt for a light. She handed him one, giving him a look. When she saw the cigar, she asked, "How long you been smoking again?"

"I haven't," he replied. "Just need it today." He got two puffs in before spotting Flaco's all-black Tahoe pulling up. They'd all packed light, so everyone managed to squeeze in and get out of busy LAX.

As they drove off, Flaco spoke up. "Sorry about your sister, Weed. I think she's being held at the MC club."

"What makes you think that?"

"I saw her bike parked behind the club myself, Weed."

Weed stared out the window, then turned back to Flaco, his voice low and serious. "Can you get me some firepower?"

"I can get a little," Flaco said, and then Crystal chimed in, "I got connections too, Weed. Give me a minute to reach out."

"Good. Flaco, can you grab a couple of ,45s, a couple of 9mms, and some ammo?"

"I'm on it," Flaco assured him.

They eventually arrived at Flaco's place in Bellflower. Weed thought it was a good spot to lay low. After Flaco left them with a shotgun and an AR-15, they all went out to the backyard to talk. Finally, Sexy was able to tell Weed why she'd called him. Before she started, though, Weed realized he hadn't checked his phone—somehow, it had been on airplane mode. He turned it off, then listened to Sexy.

"I got a call from Savage. He was ordering me to come to California."

"Well, you're here now, and he doesn't know it yet. Let's just play this by ear and see what Flaco can do to help." Everyone agreed. Weed then explained the call Terry had received from Jessie's sister, mentioning his name for the first time. When he finished, he asked who'd be down for a trip to NYC after this was handled. Everyone raised their hand.

Just then, Weed's phone buzzed—Flaco was calling. "Hello?"

"Weed, I got what you asked for, and your sister is definitely at the club."

"How soon can you get back here?"

"Give me twenty minutes. Don't want to get pulled over with all this in my truck."

"Understood. See you then."

Weed relayed the news to the crew, then they all headed back inside, each person caught up in their own thoughts. Weed was focused on taking down whoever had his sister—and Savage was at the top of the list. He also needed to text Ms. D to let her know he was okay. As soon as he finished the text, he heard a vehicle pull up in Flaco's driveway. Looking out, he saw Flaco and went out to meet him, with Doc and Pam right behind.

Once everything was inside, they checked and loaded the guns. Weed asked Flaco the total, and he replied, "$3,500." Not bad for the two .45s, two 9mms, and a couple of AR-15s. Weed then asked Flaco to explain the layout of the club where his sister was being held.

"They have a new club. It's on a corner, but I don't know all the ins and outs. Thing is, there's a Mexican bar right next to it, which could help us get in if they're connected."

Weed's mind started working on a plan. After they finished loading and double-checking the guns, they went back outside to talk strategy. The first order of business was for Sexy to call Savage and let him know she was on her way. They'd need to draw him and most of his crew away from the club, then take it from there. Everyone agreed, so they set the plan in motion.

They watched as Sexy dialed Savage's number and put her phone on speaker. A booming voice came through. "WHAT?"

"I'm gonna be in Cali in the next eight hours," Sexy said.

"Sexy, I'm not in the mood for games, woman!"

"I'm serious. I'll be there. Can I speak to my sister, though?"

"Fine. Hold on." A moment later, Tiffany's voice came through the phone.

"Hello?"

"Tiffany, it's Sexy. I'm on my way to Cali now, and I got Weed with me."

"Good, you'll need it. They're deep," Tiffany replied.

Savage came back on the line. "Alright, you talked to your sister. Now get here!"

"I'll need a ride when I land."

"Fine. Where's Crystal?"

"Last I heard, she's already in Cali."

"Alright, call when you're here." The line went dead.

Tiffany felt a surge of relief, knowing Weed was probably already in California or on the way. She'd been snatched up outside her favorite nail shop, distracted and not paying attention. One of the Deuces had walked up behind her, pressing a gun to her side and patting her down. Another grabbed her, knocked her off her bike, and dragged her into a waiting truck. They took her jacket and phone, tied her hands behind her back, and took off. When they arrived, she saw her bike parked out back and realized where they were. A guy who looked just like Snake opened the door on her side of the truck.

"Hey, T, what's up? How's your sister doing?" he asked.

"Fine, I guess," she replied.

"Well, we'll find out together soon enough." That's when she learned this was Savage, Snake's son. He'd called Sexy, demanding the money and jewels stolen from his dad and stepmom. He also wanted Crystal. Tiffany couldn't say anything then, but she felt sure Weed would come for her.

"Hey, Savage, I'm hungry. Can you get me something to eat?" she asked.

"What do you want?"

"A fat burger and some onion rings."

"Alright, I got you."

Meanwhile, Weed had Pam drop Sexy at the airport, arranging for her to return when it was time to call Savage. The rest of the crew headed to the Mexican bar next to the club to scope it out. Weed asked Flaco for additional backup, and he brought along six of his best people, two of whom knew the club's layout. Now, all they could do was play the waiting game.

CHAPTER SEVEN

They all took seats in two adjacent booths. The bar was nice, clean, and served food, with about ten Mexican locals drinking at the counter. Weed grabbed a menu, eyeing a big wet burrito. When the waitress came by, he ordered one with a lemonade. The others started picking up menus and ordering, following his lead.

One of Flaco's guys came over, introducing himself as Kevin. Weed shook his hand. "Tumbleweed," he replied, nodding for Kevin to take a seat.

"Weed, can I speak freely?" Kevin asked. Weed nodded, and Kevin continued, "We can get your sister out without causing a scene."

Weed raised an eyebrow. "How's that?"

"Move in at night. They have gatherings here every evening."

"But how will we know where my sister is?" Weed asked.

"This place only has four rooms—two restrooms, a meeting room, and a sleeping room. She's most likely in the sleeping room. I was a prospect for this club before I backed out. Savage lives up to his name—he only looks out for himself and his Sergeant at Arms, who's his cousin."

"Alright, that answers most of my questions," Weed said. "But how do we get into this club packing heat?"

"They don't check people coming to party, only patch holders. Savage has crossed so many other clubs on the West Coast that he's paranoid about who's wearing what."

Weed nodded. "None of us have a patch. We're all independent, even T."

"Good. Then we can all slip in around 8:30 or 9 tonight."

"I'm trusting you, Kevin. I also heard T's bike is in the back lot?"

"If it's there, the key's probably in it. We can grab it too."

"Alright, then," Weed said as he spotted the waitress coming over with his food. "Looks like my burrito's here." He offered some to Kevin, who declined, and mentioned he'd head back to Flaco's after everyone finished eating. Kevin suggested sending someone to keep an eye on the club just in case they moved T. Weed agreed, and Kevin said he'd ask Less, who had a friend in the Deuces, to hang out there.

"Perfect," Weed replied. "Let me know if there's any movement."

As Weed dug into his meal, he saw three Deuces walk into the bar. He nearly lost his appetite, but quickly noticed that Lil Bitt and Terry were both on point, with Lil Bitt subtly pulling her gun closer. Weed quietly moved his .45 onto his lap, feeding himself with his left hand. The Deuces took seats at the bar, ordering food, while Weed glanced over to see Doc and Pam also watching with their hands in their laps. It seemed the whole crew was ready.

The waitress brought out the rest of their food, and they all ate in peace, keeping an eye on the Deuces. They didn't finish until the Deuces had left. As soon as they were gone, Kevin returned to say that Less was on his way to the club. His friend was babysitting "a hot chick" for "The President," Savage.

"Good, Kevin. Make sure he calls if T is moved, and tell him to follow if necessary."

"We got you, Weed."

After finishing his meal, Weed walked over to where Doc and Pam were wrapping up and told them it was time to head back to Flaco's and discuss the plan for the night. They were more than ready to leave. As Doc paid the bill, Pam went over to let Terry and Lil Bitt know it was time to go.

On the way out, Weed called Sexy to check in. "Sexy, how are you doing?"

"I'm good. I've got some money on the way from one of my club brothers, and my flight's on schedule."

"What time's the money coming in?"

"It's being sent Western Line, so I'll have to pick it up at the airport."

"Alright. Call me once you've got it. What time's your flight landing?"

"7:49 p.m., Cali time."

"Got it. You might not need to stay at the airport—we have another plan in motion. Pam will meet you there."

"Alright, Weed. I'm with you all the way!"

"I'll call once we finish our meeting."

"And if the money gets here first, I'll call you," Sexy replied. They hung up, and Weed looked up as their ride pulled up to Flaco's place.

He liked Flaco's cozy two-bedroom ranch with its enclosed patio. The backyard felt secure, almost like a sanctuary. The crew gathered in the back again, this time with Kevin leading the discussion. Doc took the lead on questions, starting with how Kevin knew so much about the club. Kevin repeated what he'd told Weed earlier, word for word, about the layout and the members.

Satisfied, Doc moved on to the next big question. "How are we getting in there armed?"

Once again, Kevin laid out the plan, explaining how the Deuces didn't check partygoers, just their own patch holders. With everything clarified, Terry finally spoke up.

"I like the plan," she said, "but we don't all need to be inside the club at the same time."

Weed glanced at Doc, who nodded in agreement. "Good point," Weed said, gesturing for Terry to explain her idea.

Terry stood in the middle of the group and began outlining her plan. Just as she was about to dive into the details, Weed's phone rang. He glanced at the caller ID—it was Sexy. He held up a finger for Terry to pause and answered.

"Weed, I got the money. What do you need me to do?"

Weed checked his watch, realizing he was still on Midwest time—three hours ahead of Cali time. They only had two hours before

Sexy's flight was set to land, and they were supposed to meet at the club around the same time.

"Pam, would you mind going to pick up Sexy at the airport?" he asked.

"No problem, I'm on my way," Pam replied. Weed then told Sexy to wait where she'd been dropped off.

"I'll be there," Sexy agreed, and they hung up.

Weed turned back to Terry, nodding for her to continue with her plan.

CHAPTER EIGHT

They had two vehicles—the Tahoe and a Chevy Blazer. Terry, Lil Bitt, and Pam went into the club, which looked packed from where Weed was watching outside. Weed and Sexy were in the Blazer, sitting in the alley behind the club where bikes were streaming in and out of the back gate. Weed spotted his sister's bike parked there. Up front, Kevin, Doc, and Flaco waited in the Tahoe, ready to move in as soon as they got the all-clear from Less.

Sexy called Savage's number and put him on speaker.

"What, Sexy?" he answered.

"Did you get my text, Savage?"

"Yeah, I'm sending a ride now."

"Okay, I'll be out front."

Savage didn't bother replying; he just hung up. They waited, watching to see who would come to pick up Sexy. They all kept their hopes up that they'd get Tiffany out alive. A few minutes later, Kevin got a text from Less: three Deuces were heading out to get Sexy, and for some reason, the rest of the Deuces were moving their bikes. Kevin passed the info to Weed, who quickly texted back, asking if Tiffany was still inside. After a few minutes,

Kevin replied that Tiffany was in the sleeping room and that Savage was gearing up for a ride.

Weed messaged everyone: *As soon as Savage leaves, we move in to get Tiff!* Terry responded that she had an eye on Savage, and he looked just like his father, Snake. Weed texted back, asking if she could reach Tiffany, and she replied, *I'm on it now.*

A few minutes later, a formation of about fifteen bikes rolled out of the back gate. Weed felt a surge of relief—they could finally move to get Tiffany. As soon as Savage and his crew cleared out, Terry texted that they had eyes on Tiffany—she was in a room, hands tied to a chair. Weed asked if they could get her now and meet at the back door. Terry replied, *Two minutes.*

Weed called Doc, telling him that Sexy was grabbing Tiffany's bike, and that he'd meet the girls at the back gate. Kevin, overhearing, said that Flaco was already moving toward Weed on foot.

Doc assured him, "We've got the front covered. Be careful, partner."

"Will do," Weed replied, pulling the Blazer to the gate's entrance just as he saw the headlights of his sister's bike coming toward him. He let Sexy pass through, then quickly blocked the gate with the Blazer. Just then, Flaco ran up to him, and they both heard a rapid burst of gunfire—"Bam, bam, bam, bam!" Weed turned to see his sister, Terry, Pam, and Lil Bitt sprinting toward him, with Lil Bitt pulling up the rear. She turned and unloaded her clip with the 9mm she had. Weed rolled down the window and shouted for her to get clear. She stepped aside just in time for Flaco to open up with the AR-15, clearing the path.

Weed jumped out of the truck, flung open the door, and motioned for everyone to pile in. Just as they loaded up, a loud boom erupted from the front of the club, followed by six more. Weed pulled around front to see Doc hanging out of the Tahoe's window, firing a 12-gauge Mossberg. Kevin, in the driver's seat, flashed his headlights at Weed, then peeled off as Weed merged onto the main road.

Up ahead, he spotted Sexy, leading on his sister's bike, while Doc and Kev fired out the back of the Tahoe to ensure no one was following. They headed to the Travel Lodge in Gardena, the same spot they'd used before. This time, they parked in the alley and waited for Crystal to open the door to their room. Terry texted the room number—213. It was always a good feeling when a plan came together.

In the alley, Lil Bitt untied Tiffany before they headed upstairs. Crystal mentioned she had also gotten a room for the bike. Terry nodded toward Room 113, directly below theirs.

Weed turned to Sexy and told her to leave Tiffany's bike with him and join the others. He wheeled the bike in front of Room 113, found the door unlocked, and parked it inside, locking the door behind him. He took the key with him and headed upstairs.

When he walked into Room 213, Kevin was on the phone with Less, who was yelling into the speaker that several people had been shot near the back door and that two had been killed at the front. Kevin asked if he and his friend were okay, and Less replied that his friend had taken a bullet to the gut from one of the girls to make it look good, but other than that, they were fine.

Kevin then asked, "Did Savage get back before you left?"

"No, he's up north on a big deal. But when he gets back, he's gonna be pissed. I'll keep you updated if I hear anything," Less replied before hanging up.

Weed scanned the room, checking in to make sure everyone was alright. Just then, the bathroom door opened, and Tiffany emerged, heading straight for him with her arms open. She wrapped him in a bear hug and planted a sloppy kiss on his cheek.

“I love you, bro!”

“I love you too, Tiff. I’ll always be there for you.”

“I knew you’d come for me.”

Doc cleared his throat, bringing everyone back to the moment. Weed looked at him. “What’s the plan now?”

Doc replied, “We need to get to Vegas, scope out what we need, and wait for Savage to call Sexy so we can get a read on his next move.”

“I’m with you. But first, let’s grab some rest and hit the interstate at first light.”

Everyone found a spot to crash for a few hours. Weed asked Tiffany what she wanted to do with her bike—take it to Vegas or leave it downstairs.

“I’m riding my bike,” she replied. “The rest of you can just follow me.”

Weed chuckled, shaking his head at his sister. He scanned the room and saw Crystal watching him. He gave her a smile, then reached for his phone to call his wife, who was probably worried.

CHAPTER NINE

Savage got a call from his cousin at the club, telling him that two females had just come in, shot up the place, and took Tiffany. Ever since he was young, motorcycles and the club had been his life. His dad, Snake, had kept him on minibikes and, as he got older, on dirt bikes. After his father was killed and robbed, Savage swore he'd find the killers and get back what was stolen. Now, at 26, he looked just like Snake and was determined to handle this.

He pulled up the club's surveillance feed on his phone, watching the footage of the two women who'd stormed in and taken Tiffany. He didn't recognize either of them, but he needed to figure out who they were—and fast. He called the brothers he'd sent to pick up Sexy at the airport, asking if they'd found her. They told him she hadn't been on the flight. He hung up and returned to the club footage, catching a glimpse of Sexy riding off on her sister's bike.

He decided to call her, hoping she'd answer. When she picked up, he put her on speaker.

"Yes, Savage, what can I do for you?"

"Well, I see you got your sister's bike back."

"Why, yes, I did! Anything else you need, Savage?"

"Sexy, you know when I catch you, it's over."

"Fine. I feel the same way you do, Savage."

"Alright, Sexy, just so you know, this means war."

"Maybe so. But what does my club have to do with this?"

"It's part of you, Sexy. And you had my club shot up."

"I don't know what you're talking about, Savage. I don't know anything about that."

"Fine. This call is done."

"Later!" Sexy hung up on him.

Frustrated, Savage went back to reviewing the footage. Unfortunately, most of the people involved were too far from the cameras to identify. He was interrupted by a knock at the door. Quickly shutting off the surveillance, he let his club brother in along with their plug, who was there to deliver a load: 100 kilos of cocaine and fifty bricks of China White. The Mexicans from Arizona were always on time with better quality than what his father used to get from New York's Cuban contacts. He couldn't make a profit on the cut-down product they'd supplied, so he'd cut ties with them. Now, the only thing they had in common was the shared goal of finding his father's killers and the ones who'd robbed them.

Savage's brother-in-arms checked the goods, then nodded to him that everything was legit. Savage gave the nod to pay up. Ernesto, their contact, was always true to his word, but it still irked Savage that he couldn't deal directly. He hated the feeling that Ernesto didn't fully trust him.

Once business was handled, he knew he needed to get back to L.A. to check on his club and the brothers.

Weed

Weed wasn't thrilled with the threat Sexy had just received from Savage.

"Weed, don't let it get to you," Sexy assured him. "We'll handle it."

"It's not that I'm worried," Weed said, "but I don't like leaving L.A. with this hanging over our heads."

"The only reason I woke you up was so you could hear the call. Now let's get out of this bathroom and try to get some sleep before anyone else wakes up."

"Alright, I got you, Sexy." He checked his phone, noticing a missed text from Ms. D. She'd written that she'd been asleep when he'd called due to the time difference but that she was worried and wanted him to call as soon as he could. It was too late to call now, so he sent a quick reply, telling her he loved her and would call her later in the day.

He lay back down, managing to catch a few more minutes of shut-eye.

Savage

Back at the club, Savage was furious about how things had gone down. The police were still swarming the place, asking questions. He'd already had the product moved to an apartment they rented for this exact situation. Parking his bike out back, he felt his rage boiling over as he walked toward the club, only to be stopped by an officer.

"Your patch says President. So, you're the head of this club?" the officer asked.

"Yes, I am," Savage replied coolly.

"Alright, can you tell me anything about this shooting?"

"No, officer. I wasn't here when it happened, and we don't have problems with anyone."

"Alright, Mr. Savage. Just don't leave town anytime soon."

"Yes, sir, I'll be around if you need me."

Savage headed inside, finding his cousin, and they went to the meeting room. As he closed the door, he spoke. "Cuz, this is a big problem—this mess has brought a lot of heat."

"I know," his cousin replied, "but don't tell me you're getting cold feet."

"No, just more cautious. The last thing we need is more police."

"Agreed. We've got a lot of product to move. Can you handle getting it cooked, weighed, and ready?"

"Not a problem."

"Good. Any of our brothers get hurt?"

"Just the one who was watching the girl."

"Did he talk to the police?"

“He told them he didn’t know why he was shot or who did it.”

“Alright. Is anyone at the hospital with him?”

“His friend’s there, just a hang-around, but he’s watching him.”

“Good. Find out where his head’s at and if he needs anything.”

“On it.”

“Also, we might need to hire a hit crew. I want every one of the Ghost Riders M/C gone—especially ‘Big Sexy.’”

“I’ll make the call. I’ve heard of her. She’s got this guy everyone mentions when they talk about her—a loner called Tumbleweed.”

“Does he hold a patch?”

“Nope. He rides independent.”

“Alright, don’t worry. We’ll find him too.”

“Got it, cuz. I’ll start moving things along.” As he turned to leave, he added, “By the way, you got a call from that Cuban woman out of New York. Said to call her ASAP—she’s got questions about some woman.”

“Alright, I’ll hit her up in a bit.”

CHAPTER TEN

The Crew

The plan had gone off without a hitch. Crystal had stayed low until the perfect moment. Now, Weed felt it was time to take care of all their unfinished business, but they needed to move on to Vegas to handle the jewels and finalize some loose ends, including dealing with Jesse's sister.

"Weed, wake up! Weed, wake up!" Tiffany's voice pulled him out of a deep sleep. Hearing her voice, knowing she was safe, brought him relief. Around him, the crew was getting ready, gathering their things to hit the road. Weed raised his voice to get everyone's attention.

"Can I have everyone's attention, please?" he called out. Terry replied, "You got it, but Lil Bitt's still in the bathroom."

Once everyone was listening, Weed laid out his plan. They had a major advantage: they knew Savage and his people, but Savage had no clue who they were. Weed suggested splitting up to get everything done. Doc, Pam, and Crystal would head to Las Vegas to find a buyer for the jewels. Terry, Lil Bitt, and Tiffany would fly to New York to deal with Jesse's sister. Meanwhile, Weed, Flaco, and Sexy would stay in L.A. to take care of Savage and put an end to this back-and-forth for good.

The crew agreed; Weed's plan made sense. They spent the next two hours refining the details, deciding they'd execute everything on the same day, at the same time, a week from now on June 12th. By that day, they'd have Savage and Jesse's sister dealt with, and hopefully, the jewels sold.

The New York team planned to fly from Vegas to Indianapolis, pick up supplies, and drive to NYC. That left Tiffany in the lead for the ride to Vegas with Doc, Pam, Crystal, Lil Bitt, and Terry. Meanwhile, Flaco and Kevin were on the phone, trying to get intel on Savage's latest moves.

Needing a moment, Weed slipped into the bathroom and called his wife.

"Hello?" she answered.

"Hey, baby, how are you?"

"I'm fine, James. How are you?"

"Better now, hearing your voice."

"I miss you, James. I can't wait for you to come home."

"Just give me a week, baby, that's all I need."

"I'll be here waiting, love."

"I love you." As he hung up, Weed felt the depth of his love for her. Despite everything he'd put her through, she stood by him one hundred percent.

He moved out of the bathroom to catch Terry before the New York team left. Everyone was loading into the Chevy Tahoe Crystal had rented. Crystal stopped him.

"Weed, we really need to talk," she said.

He looked at her, "Go ahead, you've got a few minutes."

Crystal hesitated, "Not here. Just keep your phone on. I'll call when I can."

Weed promised, "It'll be on."

As she walked away, he called after her, "By the way, Crystal, when did you have a baby?"

"Eight months after you left," she replied.

"What did you have?"

"A little girl."

"Well, I'd like to meet her someday, if I make it through all this."

"We'll talk, Weed. I just need the right time."

Weed watched Crystal walk over to Tiffany, catching their conversation as he approached.

"Did you tell him about my niece?" Tiffany asked.

"I tried, but now's not the time," Crystal replied.

"She looks and acts just like him, Crystal. You've got to tell him soon."

"I know, but he's married now and seems happy."

As Weed joined them, the conversation halted. He hugged his sister, telling her he loved her.

"Ditto," she replied with a grin. He whispered in her ear, "Make sure Jesse's sister doesn't pick up the phone again in this life."

"Got it, bro," she answered.

Weed then moved to Terry. "Keep the crew safe and make sure you take the final shot."

"Already planned that. Love you, Weed."

"Love you too." Weed turned back to see Kevin approaching.

"Weed, can we talk?" Kevin asked.

Weed nodded, and Kevin told him they needed to move the vehicles away from the hotel. Both had bullet holes, so they'd be too risky to keep here.

"We have a shop that Flaco owns. They'll fix them up or scrap them," Kevin explained.

"Alright, how far is this shop?"

"Seven blocks up the street."

"Let's go," Weed replied, just as Flaco came down the steps, finishing a phone call. "Weed, you feel like riding today?"

"I'm always down for a ride. What am I riding?"

"It's a 1970 KZ 750—a real beast. Not just anyone can handle it."

Weed grinned. "Let's do it."

"We'll head to the shop first," Flaco said. "It's a low-key spot, good for now."

Weed nodded, just as Tiffany pulled up on her bike. She gave Weed and Flaco a quick "Thank you!" then sped off with her taillights disappearing down the block.

Weed waved to the crew in the Tahoe as it pulled away, then felt his phone buzz. He checked and saw a message from his friend, the doctor: *Be safe, my friend. Until this is over, much love. Weed* replied, *It's real! Let's get rich and live long!*

Another text came in from his wife*: Stay focused on what you're doing*. He smirked and texted back*, LOL, I got you, baby! Love You!* He then turned to Flaco, asking if the room was locked.

"Yeah, I got the key," Flaco replied. They rolled out, making it to the shop without any issues despite the bullet holes.

The shop was impressive—a large warehouse with low riders, motorcycles, high-end cars, foreign imports, and even a few old-school trucks. They pulled into the garage, and the crew took the trucks away immediately. Flaco led Weed over to the bikes and showed him the 750 Kawasaki. It was sleek, all black, with racing pipes and a stripped-down engine.

"Start it up," Flaco encouraged. Weed turned the key, the bike lighting up as it started with a unique zing sound. It made him do a double-take. Flaco explained, "Someone ordered it as a custom job but never picked it up. I kept it, added a few things, and race it every chance I get."

Weed asked, "Is this thing even street legal?"

Kevin chuckled, "It shouldn't be."

Then Weed heard the 1300 Suzuki that Kevin was on roar to life, idling like a heartbeat. Flaco handed Weed a full-face helmet to match the bike, and they set out, Flaco leading the way to his house.

As they hit the Harbor Freeway, Flaco and Kevin took off, nearly leaving Weed behind. Weed hit the throttle, the bike roaring as he caught up, then passed them. He thought to himself that if this bike had a price tag, he'd buy it. He was hooked.

Flaco signaled toward the next exit, and they all pulled off the highway. Raising his helmet's visor, Weed turned to Flaco and asked, "How much for this bike?"

Flaco grinned. "We'll talk after we're done with Mr. Frank Day."

Weed searched his memory for a moment. "Savage?" he asked. Flaco nodded. Weed lowered the visor and fell in line as Kevin led the way off the highway.

CHAPTER ELEVEN

Crystal

Crystal missed Weed deeply after he left her in Muncie. He'd paid her rent for a year and left her with $50,000 in an account, enough to get by. But a month later, when she missed her period, she went to the clinic and found out she was pregnant. At first, she considered not going through with it, but Tiffany convinced her otherwise, promising to stand by her through it all. She assured Crystal that her brother would step up for the baby if she told him.

What Tiffany didn't know was that Crystal had spoken to Weed before he left. He'd told her how much he loved Ms. D and how he felt he owed his loyalty to her after everything they'd been through. He'd shared his commitment to giving Ms. D the life she deserved. A couple of times after that, Crystal thought about telling Weed, but whenever she called, he remained respectful, never making a move. He'd just ask if she needed anything, and she would always say no. Secretly, she'd hoped he'd tell her things had changed with Ms. D, but every time, he'd confirm they were still together, and Crystal would lose her nerve to tell him about the baby.

Through it all, Tiffany stayed by her side, helping her raise Jazzy, her daughter. Crystal thanked God every day for her baby girl and held onto the hope that one day she could tell Weed about her. That was her silent prayer.

"Crystal? Crystal?" Pam's voice pulled her out of her thoughts. They had stopped for a break. "Are you up, Crystal?"

"Yes, I'm up," she replied, still a little groggy.

"Are you hungry?"

"Just a bit. But I really need to use the restroom first."

"Okay, we're pulling into a truck stop with a restaurant."

After using the restroom, Crystal joined everyone at the table and grabbed a menu. Just then, Pam asked a question she hadn't prepared for.

"So, Crystal, I overheard you talking to Weed about your baby. How old is she, and what's her name?"

Crystal looked to Tiffany, who stepped in to answer, "She has a little girl who looks just like her father, my brother Weed. She's turning five this year, and her name is Jazzy." Tiffany took out her phone and showed everyone a picture of her niece.

Crystal felt her heart race as she finally spoke up. "Weed doesn't know yet," she admitted, looking down.

Doc, looking surprised, asked, "Why haven't you told him? He'd want to know he has a daughter."

"The only reason I haven't told him is because he's married to Ms. D now. He's stayed loyal to her, and I don't want to come between them."

Doc nodded thoughtfully. “I don’t think Ms. D would leave him over this. She decided not to have kids because she felt this world was too corrupt, but she’d probably accept Jazzy, especially since this happened before their marriage. Weed will take care of his kid—she looks just like him.”

“Thanks, Doc. I’ll think about it when we get to the hotel in Vegas.”

Pam chimed in with an idea, “Why not just send him a picture of Jazzy now? Maybe he’ll notice the resemblance himself. You might not even have to say anything.”

Crystal thought about it. “That’s actually a good idea, Pam. I’ll do it now, and see how he reacts.”

She found her favorite picture of Jazzy on her phone, added it to a text, and sent it to Weed. She crossed her fingers, hoping he wouldn’t be upset that she hadn’t told him sooner. Looking over at Tiffany, her best friend and Jazzy’s aunt, she saw her nod in approval, which gave her a bit of comfort. Crystal smiled back, her heart pounding as she waited, hoping that Weed would call her back.

CHAPTER TWELVE

Victoria

Victoria was Jesse's sister, and she was known for her demanding nature, always trying to control people and situations. She and Weed had once dated, which was how Weed met Jesse. Now, her main focus was finding out who killed her brother and took everything valuable he had. She'd been blowing up Terry's phone, trying to track down Lil Bitt, but that wasn't going to get her anywhere. In Weed's mind, Victoria was trouble. If Jesse hadn't set him up, Jesse would still be alive, and Victoria wouldn't be a problem now. Still, he figured it might be worth calling her to get a sense of what she was planning. Maybe he could give Tiffany and the crew a heads-up if she let something slip.

He found her number in his phone and called, keeping it off speaker since he was sitting in Flaco's living room.

"Hello, Weed?" Victoria's voice came through the line.

"Yes, how are you, Victoria?"

"I'm fine, Weed, but I know you didn't call to check on me."

"True. I did have a question for you, though."

"Go ahead."

"Why did you call me on my birthday?"

"I'm looking for a woman named Lil Bitt. I met her here in New York at my brother's place. She was a dancer he liked, and I think she was involved in his death and the robbery."

"Okay, I'm sorry about your brother, but what does this have to do with me?"

"Well, I mentioned you to her, and she said she might know you."

"I can see your point now, but I don't know anyone by that name." He decided to change the subject. "So, how've you been getting by?"

"I'm handling things. Took over where my brother left off."

"So, I could spend some money with you?"

"It depends, Weed. What are you looking for?"

"Same type of arrangement I had with Jesse?"

"I can make that happen. The price has changed, though."

"That's fine. Can I send someone to see you in a couple of days?"

"Sure, just have them call me when they get to the city. You remember where my brother's house is?"

"Yeah, I think so."

"Alright, Weed. Have them call me when they're here."

"Will do. I'll be in touch, Victoria."

After hanging up, Weed noticed a notification. He'd missed a text from Sexy and Crystal. He opened Sexy's message first.

"Weed, where are you? I'm hungry."

He texted back, "What do you want?"

"Food!!" she replied.

He chuckled, then called out to Flaco and Kevin, who were in the den on their laptops. "We need to ride. Sexy's at the room, and she's hungry. Let's get her something to eat."

Flaco nodded. "I need gas, so let's stop at the station on the main street. We'll hit up Jack in the Box after."

"Sounds good."

While he waited for them to get ready, Weed opened Crystal's message. "Here's a picture of my baby girl, Jazzy." He tapped the image, and his heart skipped a beat; Jazzy looked just like his sister Tiffany.

He replied, "She's beautiful. She looks a lot like Tiff." Just then, Flaco signaled he was ready. They fueled up, grabbed food, and hit the highway back to the hotel. Weed still needed to talk to Tiffany about the change in plans, but for now, he was enjoying the ride.

Back at the hotel, they got Sexy fed, and Weed couldn't help but admire the bike he'd been riding. It was fast, handled beautifully—exactly what he wanted. He turned to Flaco again. "So, what do you want for that bike?"

Flaco grinned. "Make me an offer, Weed."

Weed thought for a moment. "How about $4,000?"

"For you? I'll take $3,000," Flaco replied, extending his hand. Weed shook it, sealing the deal.

Sexy, watching the exchange, got excited. "What kind of bike is it?"

"It's an old-school KZ 750," Weed told her.

Sexy's eyes lit up. "Can I ride it?"

Weed laughed. "I haven't even paid him yet."

Sexy reached into her bag, pulled out a stack of cash, and counted out $3,000, handing it to Flaco. "There you go. Now, can I get the title?"

Flaco smiled, but before he could respond, Kevin's phone rang. It was Lester, so he put it on speaker.

"Kev, Savage is on one right now," Lester reported. "He's getting a crew together to search the city for the female who got away and her sister. He's been watching the club cameras. Said he spotted some dude in a Blazer helping Sexy get her sister's bike out, and he thinks he saw Flaco firing at the back door. Flaco might be on his hit list."

Weed and Flaco exchanged a look, each realizing that the stakes had just gotten higher.

CHAPTER THIRTEEN

As soon as Kev hung up with Less, Weed quickly dialed Tiffany, hoping she'd be stopped somewhere to take his call. No answer. He tried Crystal's number next.

"I'm sorry, Weed," were the first words out of Crystal's mouth.

"What are you sorry for?" he asked, surprised.

"Nothing… just wanted to say sorry," she replied. "Is something wrong? Why are you calling?"

Weed told her there wasn't a problem but that he needed to update them on his progress that day. Crystal said she'd put him on speaker so everyone could hear.

"Alright, everyone, here's the deal. I spoke to Victoria—Jesse's sister. She thinks I'm still in the drug game, so I let her believe we're interested in her services. This buys us time. We've got six more days, and we'll stick to the plan."

"So, Weed, do the girls need help from me?" Doc chimed in.

"Not yet, Doc. We're holding steady, but stay ready just in case. Thanks."

"No problem," Doc replied.

Weed asked if Tiffany was nearby. Crystal explained they were on the road, nearing Arizona, and would likely stop soon to refuel. She mentioned they'd been stopped when she'd sent him a picture earlier.

"Oh, that reminds me, Crystal. Who's the father of that beautiful little girl? She looks just like my sister. What's her name?"

Crystal hesitated. "Are you sure you want to know, Weed? Her name is Jazzy."

"Yes, I'd like to know. But if it's a problem—"

"Hold on," Crystal interrupted. Weed noticed another call coming in. It was Ms. D, so he quickly took it.

"Hello, baby. Everything alright?" he asked.

"Yes, James. Your mom called. She's worried because neither you nor Tiffany have called her or your dad."

"Alright, I'll call her next. Just six more days, and I'll be home. I promise."

"Okay, James. Holding you to that," she replied with a smile in her voice. "Love you."

"Love you too," he said, hearing the line click off. Weed returned to Crystal's call.

"Hey, sorry about that," he said.

He could barely hear Crystal's soft reply. "Weed… you're the father."

He thought he'd misheard. "What was that?"

This time, her voice was steady and clear. "Weed, Jazzy is your daughter."

Stunned, Weed stared at the phone, then opened the picture she'd sent. He studied it closely—Jazzy's face was unmistakably like his and Tiffany's. He felt both happy and overwhelmed as he processed the reality of being a father. But then questions flooded his mind. How was he going to tell Ms. D? And why had Crystal waited so long to tell him?

Hearing Crystal calling his name, he brought the phone back to his ear and finally asked, "Why didn't you tell me sooner?"

"I didn't want to disrupt your marriage to Ms. D. Every time we talked, you sounded happy, and I didn't want to interfere," she explained.

"Crystal, I understand that, but this is my daughter we're talking about. I would've wanted to be part of her life. Does she know who I am?"

"Yes, Tiffany shows her pictures of you every time she visits."

"What? My sister knew and never told me?"

"I asked her not to. A few times, she threatened to tell you if I didn't, but I kept promising I would. I'm sorry, Weed. I realize I should have told you sooner. Can you give me a chance to make this right?"

"How?" he asked, feeling a mix of frustration and understanding.

"I don't know yet, but I'll figure it out if you'll let me," she replied, her voice hopeful.

"How old is Jazzy, Crystal?"

"She turned five on May 27."

Weed took a deep breath. "Alright. I'd like to meet her… as soon as all this is over."

"Of course. Whenever you're ready," Crystal promised, relieved. "Here, take down the number of the person watching her now—her name is Tracy."

Weed saved the number, thanked her, and told her he'd be in touch. After they hung up, he took a moment to process it all, then sent a quick text to Tiffany, thanking her for looking out for Jazzy. He also let her know he was upset she hadn't told him, but grateful she'd been there for his daughter.

Next, he called his mom. She picked up on the second ring. "Finally! I called Ms. D over half an hour ago. You're late, son!"

"Sorry, Mom. I just found out some news you'll want to hear."

"Oh? What is it?" she asked, intrigued.

"You're a grandma."

"Boy, stop playing with me!"

"I'm serious, Mom. I'll send you a picture of Jazzy in a minute. I gotta go now. Love you."

"Love you too, son."

As he hung up, Weed sat quietly, realizing that in six days, he had a whole new life to meet.

CHAPTER FOURTEEN

Six Days 'til Home

Flaco burst into the living room of the suite, looking agitated.

"Weed, I just got a call from Less. He said Savage is about to comb the city looking for your sister!"

Weed took a deep breath, feeling the weight of the moment. "Alright, I'm getting tired of this dude. We need to slow him down. Any idea how he's getting around?"

"I'm not sure. I can call Less and ask; he's at Savage's club right now."

As soon as Flaco had Less on the line, Weed made a snap decision. "Tell Less to leave the club immediately. I've got a different plan."

Flaco relayed the message, advising Less to clear out because the club would be gone in half an hour. Weed turned to Flaco. "Think you can get me four glass bottles for some gas?"

Flaco thought for a second. "I've got some old bottles at the shop." Weed nodded, then asked Sexy if she was up for a ride.

Sexy smiled, catching on to his plan instantly. "Definitely."

When they arrived at Flaco's shop, Sexy took the bike for a quick spin while Flaco handed Weed four old pop bottles and a gas can with a long strip of cloth. "You making them now or later?" Flaco asked, his eyes gleaming with understanding.

"Now," Weed replied, slipping the bottles into a tote bag slung over his shoulder. Sexy returned, still buzzing with excitement from her ride, and the three of them prepared to head out.

They rode quietly, pulling into a gas station on the corner near the club. Flaco went inside, returning with a blunt wrap and a lighter. They parked near the alley behind the club, and Weed moved swiftly, dousing each bottle in gasoline. The first cocktail soared toward the row of bikes parked outside the back gate, catching them instantly. As the flames reached the gas tanks, explosions followed, one after another. The second cocktail hit the back door, its wood frame igniting almost instantly.

Weed made his way to the front of the club, tossing a third bottle that burst into flames, sending thick black smoke spiraling into the air. The last bottle went flying onto the roof, shattering on impact and spreading flames that quickly engulfed the building. Inside, chaos erupted. People scrambled through the smoke, smashing windows in desperation.

Just then, Weed spotted Savage among the frenzied club members, looking every bit like his father, Snake. Shock and rage contorted his face as he watched his club go up in flames. Weed turned to Sexy and nodded, a shared understanding passing between them. "That's enough for today," she whispered.

They regrouped with Flaco and Kev, hopping back on their bikes and speeding away. The heat of the flames and the distant wail of sirens lingered in Weed's mind, knowing that the destruction would force Savage to redirect his focus. Hopefully, that would buy them some time.

As they pulled into the hotel, Weed's phone buzzed. Seeing it was Tiffany, he answered, "Hello?"

"Bro, what's going on?" she asked, sounding concerned.

"Well, a lot, actually. And yeah, I found out I'm a father too," he said, half-joking.

Tiffany laughed. "She asked me not to tell you. She was supposed to tell you herself."

He chuckled. "Yeah, Mom's seen Jazzy and apparently already thinks she looks like me."

As they entered the room, Sexy's phone went off. She glanced at the caller ID, looked at Weed, and mouthed, *Savage.* Weed gestured for her to answer, so she did, putting it on speaker.

"What the hell, Sexy?" Savage's voice boomed through the line, rage boiling over. "My club is nearly burned to the ground, and you have no idea what I'm going to do when I find you!"

Feigning innocence, Sexy replied, "What's the problem, Savage?"

He took a shaky breath, trying to regain control. "I lost almost everything in that fire. I couldn't get to my stash… the one thing my dad left me that was worth a damn."

Weed's ears perked up. *So he's got something valuable left,* he thought. He gestured to Sexy, mouthing for her to ask more.

Casually, Sexy asked, "So what was it you lost that's worth so much?"

Savage, caught off guard, answered without hesitation. "A few rare rubies and some diamonds—stuff my dad got his hands on before he was killed."

Sexy and Weed exchanged a knowing look as she continued pressing him, getting him to reveal that the jewels had been stashed in a wall safe at the back of the club. Weed filed this information away, already considering how to get his hands on Savage's hidden treasure.

After ending the call with Savage, Weed sent a quick text to Doc, instructing him to call once they'd settled in Vegas. Flaco watched Weed, his expression one of wary suspicion, as if questioning the sanity of taking this vendetta even further.

Weed grinned back, reading the question in Flaco's eyes. *Oh, yes, I'm absolutely thinking of taking him down completely.*

For the rest of the day, Weed stayed close to Flaco, keeping a low profile but not letting him out of his sight. Weed wasn't sure how Flaco would take the next move he was planning so he kept silent while his mind raced with the possibilities.

CHAPTER FIFTEEN

Five More Days 'til Home

Weed woke up early to a text from Doc, apologizing for the late response and asking what was up. Weed replied, telling him to call when he got up. After checking that everyone was still asleep, he headed to the bathroom, thinking about his plan for Savage. He needed to know if Flaco, Kevin, and Less would back him on this. His own crew was scattered, and while he didn't think he'd need the extra hands, this plan was a last-minute thing. Savage had messed with his family, and Weed was set on making him pay for his sins. With only five days left to settle everything, Weed knew he had to make sure everyone was still committed to the plan, even with this added side job.

When he came out, everyone was still asleep. Weed decided to catch a bit more sleep himself until Doc called or the others woke up. A couple of hours later, his phone finally buzzed.

"Hello?" he answered.

"Weed, what's good?" Doc asked.

"Doc, you in the mood for some fun and extra cash?" Weed replied.

"I'm always up for fun and money, my friend. What do you have in mind?"

"Well, Sexy got some info from Savage that could be useful for our future 401K."

"Oh yeah?" Doc chuckled. "Tell me more."

"Turns out Savage is sitting on more than we thought. He's got some valuables that would fit nicely with what we already have in play."

Doc's voice perked up. "Need me to come back to L.A.?"

"No rush," Weed assured him. "Just keep your phone on and some gas in your truck."

"Got it. And sis?"

"She's sleeping. Guess she and Crystal hit the slots last night and ran into someone from the past. Sounds like it was all good, though."

"Interesting," Doc replied. "Let me know when you need me, Weed. I'm with you."

"I'll keep you posted," Weed promised.

Weed noticed Flaco stirring on the floor nearby and gestured to him. "Flaco, got a minute to talk?"

"If it's about Savage, we don't have to go outside," Flaco said, sitting up. "We'd already planned on hitting him after you got your sister back. That's why I gave you that look."

"So, what's the move?" Weed asked.

Flaco smirked. "I'm not greedy, Weed. We can go 50/50 right down the middle."

"Sounds fair to me," Weed replied, nodding.

"Also, Savage has three drug houses, plus a big stash house out by Paris Lake with all the cash and goods. He's holding more than he mentioned."

Weed raised an eyebrow. "You know this for sure?"

Flaco nodded and dialed Less, putting him on speaker. After a few rings, Less's voice came through.

"What's good, Flaco?"

"How's it going with watching Savage?" Flaco asked.

"He's loaded, no doubt. I'll get you the exact address out by Paris Lake. I'm riding up with Heavy tomorrow to check it out."

"Good. Keep me posted," Flaco said. "Send a few pics if you can."

"Will do."

Flaco hung up and turned to Weed, who nodded in agreement. They were on the same page. Sexy started stirring, noticing the exchange.

"Weed, sounds like a good deal. Let's do it," she said, catching on.

Weed shook his head, smirking. "Some things never change."

"I told you I'd always have your back, Weed," Sexy replied with a grin. Flaco glanced at Kevin and laughed, "Looks like it's all set."

As they got ready for the day, Weed knew he'd need to get a hold of his sister to make sure they were still on track. He also needed to check in with his wife to see where they stood after Jazzy's reveal. But first, he dialed Tiffany, hoping to catch her.

When she didn't answer after three tries, Weed called Doc back instead.

"What's up, Weed?"

"I've been trying to reach sis, but no answer."

Doc reassured him, "I just left her room. She's still sleeping, same as Terry. Don't worry, we're all set over here."

"Good to hear. I'll be in touch soon."

"Ok, cool!"

CHAPTER SIXTEEN

Four Days 'til Home

Weed didn't get the chance to talk to his sister like he'd planned because she and Terry had slept all day. He knew they'd be flying from Vegas to Indianapolis this morning, so he'd need to talk to her once she touched down in Naptown. He still hadn't worked up the courage to tell his wife about Jazzy, but he figured he'd try again today. Meanwhile, they were still holed up in the hotel room waiting for Less to send the pictures of Savage's stash house, and Weed was hoping Savage's setup was as predictable as his father's had been.

Kevin broke the silence, mentioning he was hungry. Sexy chimed in, saying she could eat too. Weed realized he hadn't had anything since yesterday either, so when Flaco suggested ordering pizza to avoid leaving the room, everyone agreed. Sexy made the call, and right after, Flaco's phone rang. Seeing that it was Weed's sister, Flaco answered on speaker.

"What's up, Tiff?"

"Is my bro around?" she asked.

Weed called out, "I'm right here, sis!"

"Where do you want me to go first?"

"Head to my place first," Weed told her. "I already talked to Ms. D. The rental car's under the name Paul Wright, out on High School Road, all paid for. Just call when you're ready to get on the highway to NYC."

"I will, Bro. The view up here is amazing, by the way."

"You're calling me from the plane?" Weed laughed.

"Yep! I'll call when I touch down."

As she hung up, Sexy confirmed the pizza order, and Weed, ready to give up on Less's call, decided to hit the shower. While he was getting ready, Flaco received a text, and when he opened it, a series of photos of a large, pristine house popped up on his screen. Weed examined the shots closely, noting the street sign and address. Flaco explained that this house was supposedly where Savage kept everything, though he wasn't sure about the security setup.

"What's the plan for this spot?" Weed asked.

Flaco suggested they all take a ride to the house, check it out together, and see what they were dealing with. Weed looked over at Sexy for her take.

"Weed, we're down to four days. We still have Savage and Jesse's sister to handle. Let's take a look, but we can't afford to spend too much time unless we're sure this is worth it."

"I hear you," Weed said, nodding.

Once they were done eating, they prepared to head out. As they got to Weed's bike, he looked over at Sexy. "You gonna ride with me or make me ride on the back?"

She laughed, agreeing to take the back on the way there if he promised to switch on the way back. As she climbed on, she tightened her grip on his waist and whispered, “Weed, I don’t trust Kevin. Something about him seems shady.” Weed noted her concern—she hadn’t steered him wrong before.

They hit the 110, picking up speed, and Weed gave Sexy a quick tap to signal they were riding fast. They reached Flaco and Kevin, who were keeping pace, and for a moment, the California breeze and perfect weather almost made Weed think about staying longer. But with his wife back home, he knew that was just a passing thought—especially with the news he still had to break to her.

After about 45 minutes, Flaco signaled for an exit. Kevin mentioned he needed gas, so they stopped nearby to fuel up. Weed took a moment to check his phone, seeing a message from Tiff saying she was about to land in Naptown. He responded that he’d make sure Ms. D had everything they needed. As he looked over his texts, he found one from his wife, “I love you and hope you’re staying focused on your mission.” He chuckled, replying, “Love you too. Tiff’s on her way to you; she’ll need a few things before she heads to NYC.” He hoped his message would be enough to get Tiff all the support she needed.

Back on the road, they soon exited the highway and parked about three blocks from the house. Flaco called Less, who said he was still at the house and would send more info soon. Weed suggested they ride past to get a closer look.

As they approached, Weed saw a large, well-kept home, blending seamlessly with the neighborhood. Several bikes and a clean, classic 1957 Chevy truck were parked out front. Weed noticed a small camera hidden on the front of the house. He quickly signaled everyone to keep moving, not wanting to draw attention.

They pulled over a few blocks down, where Flaco received another text from Less. The message confirmed that the house had cameras and two safes inside, guarded by only three workers who weren't heavily armed. Weed smirked, realizing Savage must have felt pretty secure with this house's hidden location.

"We could score big here," Weed said, "but I don't want any of the drugs."

Flaco replied, "We'll handle the drugs and split the rest." They shook on the deal, and Weed glanced at Sexy, who nodded toward Kevin as if to remind him of her earlier warning. Weed kept her concerns at the forefront of his mind as they all mounted up to head back to the hotel. It was getting late, and Weed still needed to check in with his sister and the rest of the crew. With only three days left, he planned to bring everyone home and finally get everybody paid just like he'd promised.

CHAPTER SEVENTEEN

Three Days 'til Home

By the time they got back to the hotel, the evening air had cooled off. Weed had given Sexy his jacket for the ride since she was only wearing shorts and hadn't brought one. His long-sleeve shirt was enough to keep him comfortable, and he knew the extra layer was good to have in case he fell, he had done that before and knew that road rash was not to be played with.

As they pulled into the lot, Weed felt an urgency to relieve himself and asked Sexy for the room key. He hurried up the stairs, but as he went to unlock the door, it creaked open on its own. Instinctively, he stepped back, drawing his pistol, and signaled to Sexy and Flaco that something wasn't right. Flaco was quick to pull his own gun, while Sexy positioned herself behind Kev, eyeing him warily. She hadn't fully trusted him from the start, and Weed knew if Kev tried anything, she'd be on him in an instant.

Weed nudged the door open a little further, cautiously scanning the darkened room. He moved toward the bathroom and flipped on the hall light, casting a glow that revealed the room had been ransacked. Their belongings were scattered everywhere, and it was clear someone had gone through everything. Weed checked the room, finding no one inside, and called for Sexy and Flaco to come in.

Sexy called out that the manager was on his way up. As Weed and Flaco stowed their guns, the manager—a dignified older man in traditional Indian attire—entered, apologizing profusely for the break-in. He explained in careful English that they had video footage of the incident if it would help.

Weed asked if he'd called the police, but the manager admitted he'd had a feeling to consult with them first. He then offered a new room, free of charge, if they wanted to stay. Sexy suggested they check the video footage before deciding, and Weed agreed.

Following the manager to his living quarters, they met his wife and daughter, who Weed recognized from the office window. In the living room, they watched as the manager's daughter pulled up the footage, showing two Mexican Americans breaking into the room. Weed felt a sense of relief knowing who he was dealing with, and they all agreed to take the new room for the night. The manager's daughter informed them that the intruders were locals in the area, and they thanked her for the tip. The new room was just two doors from the office, offering more security. Weed shook hands with the manager and thanked him before they returned to gather their belongings.

It turned out that the intruders hadn't taken much—just an outfit from Weed's bag and about $18,000 he'd left there. Sexy lost $300, but they laughed when she revealed they hadn't found the stash she'd hidden in her Bro. Once they were settled in the new room, Weed checked his phone and saw five new messages, two of which caught his eye immediately—one from Victoria and the other from his sister. He opened Tiff's message first, which read, "Having a little trouble with the rental car, so I'm a little behind on our time table, but trust me, I'm on it Bro!"

Weed replied, asking if he could call her, and while he waited, he checked Victoria's message, confirming she was ready to move forward with the deal. He messaged her back, saying he'd be ready within 24 hours. Next, he read the message from Ms. D: "I love you, James. Stay focused on your business and hurry home! They are having a problem with the car." Right then, his phone rang—it was Tiff.

"Hello, Bro?"

"What's good, sis?"

"The guy we usually use for cars is locked up at the moment."

"Alright, can you get one to Cleveland, Ohio? I've got a friend who might be able to help from there."

"Yeah, I'll get a legit car for now and hit the road."

"Sounds good, sis. Oh, and Victoria's ready for you. I told her within 24 hours. We need to make at least two buys before we handle business. She'll likely skip the first but will want to show up for the second—she's greedy like that."

"Trust me, I know, Bro. Heading to get a car now. Ms. D has set us up with what we need at your place."

"Alright. Love you, sis. Talk soon."

After hanging up, Weed read the next text from Doc: "Weed, we are good for a small buy from the Arabs on some of the product." He replied, "It's a start. Once they see it's real, we'll get the rest off to them for sure."

Lastly, he read a message from Crystal: "Weed, I'm sorry for not telling you about Jazzy. You did have the right to know." He texted back, "It's cool. I forgive you. As long as I live through this to see her and help raise her, I'm good."

There was a knock at the door. Weed and Flaco both drew their pistols while Sexy slipped into the bathroom. Kev opened the door to find the manager's daughter. Weed motioned for her to come in, and she went straight up to him.

"It seems like you're the leader here," she began, not waiting for a response before continuing, "My father has great respect for you. He remembers you from the last time you stayed here a long time ago." She paused, locking eyes with Weed. "You took down Snake, the leader of the bike club that killed my uncle—my father's brother. For that, he respects you deeply." She stepped forward, emBroced him, and whispered, "Thank you," before quietly leaving the room.

Weed looked over at Flaco, who wore an expression of shock. He hadn't known they were the ones who took down Snake, and the look on his face was priceless. Weed just nodded, realizing they were one step closer to finishing this—and one day closer to getting home.

CHAPTER EIGHTEEN

2 Days 'til Home

The rest of the night went smoothly, with no unexpected visitors, and Weed managed to get some solid sleep. In the morning, his phone had been buzzing nonstop with missed calls from his sister. Remembering he hadn't called his guy Rob in Cleveland to help her and Terry get a car, he decided to make it his first priority.

He called his sister first, and she picked up quickly, sounding a bit annoyed.

"Bro, did you spend the night with Sexy or something?"

He laughed. "No, sis, just needed a reset. Are you and Terry okay?"

"Yes, we're fine, but a little grimy from the road."

"Alright, give me a minute. I got you."

Weed scrolled through his contacts until he found Rob's number. Rob was reliable—a big, smooth-talking, light-skinned guy from the Heights, married to Jodi, who was a solid ten. Weed called, and Rob answered on the second ring.

"What's good, Weed?"

"Rob, my sister's in town and needs a car to get her to New York and back. Think you can help?"

"I've got just the thing. She can leave it wherever when she's done. It's $500 with plates on it."

"That works." Weed called his sister back, gave her Rob's info, and told her to call him when she was on her way.

With the room to himself, Weed figured he'd make the most of the quiet time, so hurried to the bathroom to release his hurting stomach and take a quick shower, but as he came out of the bathroom, the manager's daughter was there, standing in the middle of the room, wearing nothing. In reaction, Weed's manhood jumped to attention. She said, "I see you are happy to see me?"

Weed could not hide that fact. He then asked her how she knew he was in there alone.

She answered, "I saw them when they left. They said something about going to Flaco's house for something and stopping to get something to eat on the way back. They've only been gone now about 20 minutes, so if you hurry I can take care of that problem you have right there real fast."

Without thinking, he fell for the lust. The whole time, he felt like his wife was going to walk through the door any minute. She did not lie, though. She took care of him real quick. She laid him back on the bed and rode him like she was riding a horse. He felt his eyes roll back into his head as she was riding him. Then when she rose her head up to kiss him, they both released at the same time. She laid her body on top of him for a moment to get herself together and he took the time to do the same. He hadn't planned it, but he let the moment happen, feeling a strange mix of thrill and guilt. Afterward, she thanked him, wrapped herself up, and left the room, promising that his secret was safe with her. Weed made sure the door was locked, took another shower, and then sat down to clear his head. He had all kinds of thoughts running through his head, so he hurried in the shower, got back in room, got dressed, and tried to clear his head the best he could. With everything being on time thus far, he was ready to get back to his home and finish chilling and living the laid back life that he was living in Naptown.

He figured it was as good a time as any to touch bases with the rest of the crew since he was still alone. He texted Doc and asked him what was good on his end. He texted his wife and asked how she was doing today. Then he texted Sexy and asked how long before they would be back to the room.

Weed started his morning off by catching up on his messages. Doc's text had him dialing immediately.

"Weed, we pulled in $30 million from half the jewelry sale to the Arabs, but they're asking questions we can't answer," Doc said.

"Do you need some family out there for protection?" Weed asked.

"Yes, I need to get this cash out of my hands, fast."

"Alright, I'll send Sexy to handle it. She's close and can pick up a rental right away. Sit tight, Doc; it'll be handled within the hour."

"Perfect. Thanks, Weed."

Weed hung up, feeling the gears turning for today's tasks. Next, he reached out to his wife, suggesting she take a week off and join him in Vegas, booking a rental car to drive back. Her excitement to see the city had her agreeing without hesitation, and she promised to call when everything was set.

Once he was ready, he called his sister to check on her status. "Sis, everything go smooth with Big Rob?"

"Yeah, he set us up solid, and we're already on the road," she said.

"Good to hear. Stay safe and hit me if you need anything."

A call from Victoria then interrupted his planning.
"I've got to handle some trouble in Philly, but your people will still get what they need," she informed him.

"Good. Just know if this product's as solid as before, I'll be back with at least half a mil for you."

"Looking forward to it, Weed."

Weed put the phone down, getting another text from his wife with her flight details. She'd be touching down in Vegas at 3 a.m. He forwarded the details to Doc, satisfied that things were finally coming together.

The door opened as Sexy, Flaco, and Kev came back in.

"What's up, Weed?" Sexy asked, handing him a heavy steak burrito.

Weed thanked her, tearing into the wrapper and savoring his meal. As he ate, Flaco reminded him they needed to get going to keep watch on Savage's stash house. Weed agreed but still took his time enjoying the meal, knowing it would be a long day. He checked in with Doc to confirm that the cash was secured, and Doc reassured him that it was already taken care of. His last text was to his wife, double-checking her travel schedule.

Everyone was ready to roll when Kev, looking out the door, suddenly motioned for them to hold up. “Something’s up,” he said. Sexy peeked out, then called for Weed, who quickly joined them. Down the hall, two familiar faces—Mexican guys from the security footage—were attempting to break into a room. Weed had an idea, telling Sexy he’d circle around through the bathroom window to catch them by surprise. He’d signal her when he was ready, and they’d move in together. Weed climbed out the bathroom window, ran along the fence, and got into position near the room, gun in hand.

Once the men entered, he signaled Sexy. She, Flaco, and Kev rushed in. Flaco kicked the door open, and the three stormed inside, catching the intruders off guard. Weed entered just in time to see punches flying as the Mexicans struggled against Kev. Flaco raised his gun, commanding everyone to freeze. Weed moved swiftly, delivering a quick pistol whip to one of the men’s faces, knocking him out cold.

At that moment, the manager and his daughter appeared in the doorway. Weed and Sexy looked at them, waiting to see their response. The manager’s daughter calmly approached, pulled out a razor, and without hesitation, slit the throat of the conscious man. She then moved to the unconscious one, finishing him off the same way. The manager nodded approvingly at his daughter, who wiped her blade and stepped back.

Weed glanced at Flaco, gesturing toward the bodies.
“Don’t worry. I’ll handle cleanup,” Flaco assured him, pulling out his phone.

The manager’s daughter approached Weed. “Thank you,” she said softly. “If you ever need anything, I’m here for you.”
“Thanks, but I don’t even know your name,” Weed replied.
“Elizabeth,” she said, offering a slight smile before leaving.

Sexy came up beside Weed, an unmistakable edge to her voice as she eyed him suspiciously, her intuition kicking in. "What's going on with her, Weed?"

He shrugged, stepping over the bodies, ignoring his burning conscience, and heading to their room to grab his jacket and helmet. They needed to make their move on Savage's house today. As he was ready to leave, the others followed, gathering their things for the trip.

Sexy, visibly irritated, fell into step behind Weed. He put on his helmet, suppressing a smirk on his face from sensing her jealousy of Ms Elizabeth.

"Weed, we need to talk when we're done for the day," she said sharply.

"Okay," he replied, turning to nod at Elizabeth, who watched them from the manager's window, her eyes following him seductively and waving at him as they rode away.

Following Flaco toward the stash house, Weed let himself relax into the rhythm of the road, knowing he had to stay sharp. With everything going on he really was looking forward to the ride this time because he needed to relax his mind and body and a good ride always did that for him. Sexy held him tight, signaling exactly where her thoughts were heading as she rubbed him in his private area, bringing him to full attention. He knew then what was on her mind but gave her the signal to hold on because he was ready to ride!

CHAPTER NINETEEN

1 Day 'til Home

The night dragged by slowly, with not much movement around the house. For the first time, they got a clear look at Savage himself. Weed had to keep batting away Sexy's advances and her endless questions about Elizabeth. He had two hours until Ms. D would be landing in Vegas, around 3 a.m. Cali time, ready to handle the money after a couple of days in "Sin City." Tiff had already touched down in NYC, waiting to pick up the first package before making the next move. With everything starting to fall into place, Weed knew he needed a hot meal and a few hours of real rest.

Kev and Flaco had been scoping out the house, trying to figure out a way to disable the cameras so they could break in unnoticed. After hours of no luck, and with the late hour weighing on them, they decided to head back to the hotel. Weed's mind was still racing, trying to plot out the next 24 hours, knowing they had to move quietly and quickly to avoid bringing the law down on them.

Sexy kept trying to press up against him, running her hand along his thigh, but he tapped her side to signal he was about to ride hard. She tapped him back, letting him know she was ready. He hit the throttle, launching the bike like a rocket, lifting the front wheel slightly off the ground as they shot down the road. It wasn't long before they pulled up at the hotel, and Weed was beyond ready to call it a night.

When they got back to the hotel, Weed's focus was all business, but Elizabeth was waiting at the door. "That little mess I cleaned up for you is all taken care of. I just wanted to thank you and your crew for what you did for us, Mr. Weed," she said, looking him straight in the eye. Her sincerity was clear. "If you need anything, you know what I mean," she added, glancing meaningfully, "just call the office."

Weed looked her in the eye, seeing the genuine gratitude there with a little flirtation added to the mix. "You're welcome," he replied, nodding respectfully trying to keep his cool.

Sexy slid up beside him and added, "You're welcome from me too," before walking into the room. Elizabeth's eyes lingered on Weed. "If you ever need anything," she said, her voice dropping a bit, "you know where to find me."

"Sure thing," Weed replied, waiting until she walked back to the office before heading inside. Sexy followed him, throwing a warning look at Elizabeth as they passed. Once he was settled in a chair, he pulled out his phone to take care of business. His first call was to his sister, seeing as she'd left a missed call.

"What's up, sis?"

"Bro, we got the first package off two of her goons. Everything's correct. What's the next move?"

"I need to call Rob, see if he's got a buyer lined up. I'll hit you back once I know."

"Hey, she gave me eight kilos, though."

"You only paid for six! I'll need to call her, too."

"Alright, we'll head toward Ohio while you handle that."

"Cool. Love you, sis."

"Love you too, bro."

Weed looked around the room, seeing everyone was either on their phones or sleeping. Sexy was lying down, looking like she was waiting for him to finish business so she could become his business. To keep his mind right, he decided to call his wife. She picked up on the second ring.

"Hey, baby," she greeted him, her voice warm.

"How are you, baby?"

"I'm good. That plane ride wore me out, though."

"Call Doc to find out where your room is, and once you're all settled, call me back?"

"Will do. By the way, James, I already won $300 on the slots here."

He chuckled, "Good job, but don't give it all back to them, alright?"

"I won't baby." She laughed.

They hung up, and Weed turned to call Big Rob in Ohio.

"Weed, I was expecting your call," Rob answered on the first ring.

"Yeah, my sister's on the way to you with eight."

"What's the price?"

"$29,000 each, but I'll give you $20,000 each if you take all of 'em."

Weed nodded, "More than fair. I'll let her know they're coming to you."

After ending the call, he immediately hit up his sister again, and Terry picked up.

"What's up, Weed?" she asked.

"All set with Rob; he'll give you $20,000 each. You two get there safe, alright?"

"Got it. Your sister's handling it, but she's been off since those tacos," Terry added, laughing.

Weed chuckled and said, "Glad it's all good." He then dialed Victoria but got no answer, so he leaned back, deciding to wait for her call. Just as he started to close his eyes, his phone buzzed—it was her.

"Weed, I was just about to call you," she said.

"You sent a couple extras?"

"Yes, that's on me. Thought you deserved it."

"Good to know. We'll be ready in a day or so. Got a quarter mil here waiting. Sound good?"

"I'll be there myself to collect."

When Weed hung up, he felt satisfied, knowing she'd fall right into the setup. He leaned back, closing his eyes for a moment, but Elizabeth's face flashed in his mind—her warm, brown skin, her scent that still lingered. He felt himself start to drift when his phone buzzed again. It was Ms. D.

"James, what's this setup you got me in?" she asked, her tone questioning.

"Baby, you're set to enjoy Vegas for a couple of days. Relax."

"So I get a room with a safe, hang out, and then drive back in two days?"

"That's it, my queen. And take an extra thousand from me."

She laughed, "Alright, I'll text you the room number. Love you, James."

"Love you too, baby. Be safe."

Just as he drifted off, Flaco woke him up. "Weed, we just got the break we needed. Less will be in the house all day tomorrow. Two of Savage's guys are brothers, and their mom passed, so they're leaving for funeral arrangements."

Weed's eyes lit up. "What time?"

"Most of the drop-offs happen late in the afternoon, so 4 p.m.?"

"Perfect. Let me hit up my sister, see if she can hit Victoria at the same time."

Weed called Tiff, and Terry answered.

"Everything good?" he asked.

"Yep, just at some hole-in-the-wall off the highway, resting after leaving Rob."

"Cool. How'd that go?"

"Paid in full," Terry confirmed.

"Great. Tomorrow, we're hitting Savage at 4 p.m. Can you handle Victoria at the same time?"

"We got you, bro," Terry assured him.

With that settled, Weed called Doc next, who answered right away.

"We're about to clear out of here, Weed. Buyers are eager, but my gut's saying don't trust them with everything right now."

"Cool. Give the cash to Ms. D, then head back here, alright?"

"You got it," Doc replied.

Weed turned to Sexy, who was still on the phone with Savage, nodding to let him know she'd set up a meet for tomorrow. He caught her eye and gave her a nod, signaling he'd handle things with Kev. Everything was finally coming together, and all that was left was his final call to Ms. D.

"Baby, Doc's on his way with the money for you. Just load up and be safe, alright?"

"I'm on it, James. I'll call you once I'm out of Vegas."

As Weed ended the call, a feeling hit him. He needed to check with Victoria one last time. He went to the bathroom, letting the phone ring. She picked up on the second ring.

"Weed, I was just about to call you," she said.

"Oh yeah? What's up?"

"Small change of plans, Weed. I need another day, some issues with my plug."

"Another day, huh? I can wait that long."

"Thank you. I'll deliver it personally when we're ready," she promised.

After hanging up, he knew she'd be walking right into his trap.

CHAPTER TWENTY

24 Hours to Home!

When Weed came out of the bathroom, he kept quiet about Victoria's delay. He had already agreed with Flaco to keep their own people out of the robbery, so now he just needed to lock in a plan for the next day. Sitting down, he turned to Flaco.

"Flaco, what's the plan for tomorrow? How many of your crew are we using?" he asked, giving Sexy a look as if to say, *"I've got Kev under control. Don't trip."*

Then he listened to Flaco.

Flaco looked thoughtful, then asked, "What do you think is the best approach, Weed?"

Kev interrupted, "I think we should let Less and his crew handle it from the inside. We wait for the signal, then we just come in to grab whatever's in the house."

Weed exchanged a glance with Sexy and Flaco, who both shook their heads slightly. Ignoring Kev, Weed turned to Sexy. "When and where are you supposed to meet Savage?"

She replied, "He wants to meet near a restaurant close to the house. He'll probably be around there before we even arrive."

Weed replied "Ok, Flaco, we need to put someone on Savage, now, that you trust and to stay on top of him, 'cause Less cannot be in two places at once."

Flaco said, "Kev, can you find out where Savage is now and get on top of him and not lose him?"

"Yes, Flaco, I got you. I'm on it now!"

Weed looked over to Sexy and she smiled back at him. Weed then asked Flaco how many people he had ready to make this move. Kev spoke up again and said that they only need three. Weed looked over to Sexy and just shook his head. He asked Flaco again for his opinion. This time Flaco said, "What do you think Weed?"

Weed told him that they needed to wait and ask Less when Flaco texts him. Flaco agreed with this. He texted Less and waited for a reply.

Kev stood up a minute later and said, "Savage is at the club now and will be for a few. I'm headed over to the club now, ok Flaco?"

Right then, in that moment, Weed made up his mind to put everything on hold for one day and then execute his plan, 'cause Sexy was right. Something was not right about Kev. He waited for Kev to put on his riding gear and leave before he spoke another word. As soon as he heard Kev's bike leave the lot, he looked out the window to make sure he was gone and then he spoke, "Flaco, what's up with Kev?"

"What do you mean, Weed?"

"How well do you trust him, Flaco?"

"Well, we have rode together for over three years, but as far as hitting a lick together this is the first time, we've really got down like this."

Weed then looked over to Sexy and she said, "Weed, we can hit Savage tomorrow and save the lick for the day after 'cause everyone will be focused on him being killed."

Weed thought about it for a minute and said, "Ok, let's do it and call him and tell him you have found Crystal and change the meeting place for somewhere closer to the club far away from the house and that Kev does not know. Nobody knows but us and the only people for the hit will be us and Doc and Less. Flaco, you can have all the drugs and we still split the money 50/50, that way Less gets taken care of too. Cool?"

"Not a problem, Weed. I'm down to ride with you 'til the wheels fall off!"

Weed got a text from Doc and his wife at almost the same time. They both said they had left Vegas. He called his sister now that the air was clear about Kev and told them that Victoria was not meeting them until the next day. Terry was mad. Tiffany was happy because she said she needed another day to get her stomach together. Weed laughed at her and told her he loved her and hung up the phone with her. At the same time, Sexy was on the phone with Savage. He heard her tell him that she found Crystal for him and asked him if he could meet her somewhere closer to the club? Weed did not hear the answer that he gave, but he heard Sexy respond that she would find the place and meet him still at 4:00pm. Then she hung up. Flaco asked Sexy where Savage wanted to meet her and she said at a soul food restaurant on Florence and Normandy. Flaco then asked Sexy if she wanted to ride with him to go and take a look at the location to see how this was going to work. Sexy agreed. Weed asked if they could get some food from the place if it was open 'cause he could use something to eat. Sexy got up from the bed and got her riding gear on as did Flaco when he got off of the floor. Weed really wanted another bite of the forbidden fruit of Elizabeth. He was wondering if she would be awake at this time of the morning. He waited for both of them to get everything they needed for the trip. He even gave them money for the food. He walked out of the room with them to the bikes and looked over to the office after they started the bikes. There was Elizabeth, looking out through the glass from the office at them. He looked her in the eyes and she nodded her head at him. Sexy told Weed before she left not to do anything that she would not do. He kissed her on the forehead before she put her helmet on and then stood there and waited for them to pull off.

As soon as they were gone, he hurried to the room, got undressed and headed to the shower. He made sure the door to the room was unlocked and took his 45 into the bathroom with him just in case someone other than Elizabeth came into the room. He wanted her in the shower, to see the water run off of her golden brown skin. He longed to see her jet black hair pulled back away from her face. Like clockwork, he looked out of the shower through the mirror and saw her coming into the room. She pulled the native silk wrapping off with nothing on underneath. He instantly got fully erect and she hurried to the shower after she looked into the room and did not see him. He pulled the shower curtain open for her and she got in and grabbed his manhood with one hand and placed the other hand behind his neck and pulled his face to hers. She thrust her tongue in his mouth and massaged his manhood at the same time. He turned her to the water and got her whole body wet. Just as he was doing so, she turned her head and he kissed her deeply. She moaned on his tongue and he felt her body shake, as he touched her breast with both of his hands and pulled on her nipples. She broke the kiss and asked him to please fuck her now because she was not sure of how much time they had. He bent her over, facing the back wall away from the water and slowly pushed himself inside of her. She moved each time he went he went a little deeper into her, until he was fully inside of her. He then slowly moved in and out of her as she moved from side to side. He then felt her juices coming down on him and they were hot. He felt himself twice try to cum inside of her, each time stopping his movement to prolong the feeling to keep up with her until finally she started to beg him to cum inside of her.

He pulled out of her and sat on the edge of the tub and sat her on top of him. She bucked when she moved like it was a lot for her to take from the top, which made him want to cum now inside of her tight pussy even more. As soon as he felt her body shake again and felt her hot juices again on his manhood, he just let loose inside of her. She moved her hips back and forth until he was totally done inside of her. He went to reach for her to bring her closer to him, but not before she reached down and grabbed his manhood and put it in her mouth. As she got him hard again, she pulled him out of the shower and put a towel on the floor. She pulled her legs almost behind her head, laying on her back and he saw nothing but all wet, pink pussy that he had to kiss this time. He licked her clit until he felt her cum. Then with her holding her legs in the air behind her head, he thrust himself inside of her and she took it all with a moan. He slow stroked her until she could not take it anymore and then he turned her over and put her on all fours and fucked her like she asked him to, deep, hard, and fast. They both climaxed together this time and then his phone went off.

He had to at least check his phone because he had too much going on at this time. He moved away from her and went for his phone. It was Sexy, so he did not answer it right then. He looked at Elizabeth and told her that he was going to have to call this person back as soon as he caught his breath. She said OK. She smiled and whispered, "Whatever you want, Weed, I'm here for you." They lingered in silence for a moment before she got dressed and slipped out of the room with a knowing smile. He told her he would try his best to do the same for her.

He caught his breath taking a moment to reflect on what had just went down and then picked up his phone to call Sexy back.

"What's up, Weed. The restaurant is open and they are serving breakfast. What would you like?"

"How about some eggs, bacon, sausage, pancakes, hash browns, and a large orange juice? Well, forget the juice. You are on the bike and you only have your back pack."

"Yes, that is true, Weed. I can get you everything else though."

"Ok, cool. I'll see you in a few?"

"Yes, you will. Is everything ok, Weed?"

"Yes, I'm cool. I just need to shower now and nap until you guys get back."

"Ok, Weed, we got you! Later!"

"Later!"

He hung up with Sexy. He saw that Elizabeth was getting dressed to leave so he got up off of the bed from where he was sitting and walked over to her. She had her back to him. He asked if she was ok. She turned to face him and said she was fine. She kissed him and left the room.

He went to the shower and his mind was on everything that had taken place the first part of the day. He noticed that Less had not gotten back with Flaco before he left with Sexy. He was really not feeling Kev anymore, so he needed to find a way around all of this and still keep everyone safe and happy.

He knew he needed to make a move and fast, so he hurried and washed himself and dried quickly, got his clothes on, and made a call to his wife to make sure she was ok.

"Yes, James?"

"Baby, I'm just calling to make sure you are doing ok?"

"I'm just fine, just driving."

"Ok, hit me when you stop."

"I will, James. Stop worrying, I'm a big girl!"

"Ok, baby, I love you!"

"Love you too!"

Then the phone went dead. He texted Doc and asked him to call him ASAP. He turned the TV on while he was waiting to hear from him. A minute later, his phone rang and it was Doc.

"What's good, Weed?"

"Can you talk, or are you driving?"

"I can talk. Pam is driving."

"Ok, cool. First off, things are not right with Flaco's friend Kev. Sexy said she does not trust him."

Doc cut him off, "The last time she told you this, you ended up killing that person."

"Yea, well, it is the woman's intuition thing I guess, Doc."

Weed takes a moment to finish telling Doc the rest of what was going on with Kev and Doc then asked what they were going to do now. He told his friend that they were just going to do it all themselves and just give Flaco 50% of what they get out of the house and he needed to make sure that Savage is done for.

"I got you, Weed. We are only two hours away from you now."

"Ok, cool. I better get myself together 'cause Savage is done for as of today. If Flaco has not gotten back to me with word from Less, we are hitting the house tonight as well."

"I got you, Weed. I got you!"

"Later, Doc."

"Later, Weed."

Weed checked his .45, ensured it was loaded with one in the chamber, switched the safety on, and laid back on the bed. He must've drifted off because he woke to the smell of breakfast filling the room. Rolling over, he looked up to see Sexy holding out a tray with his food. He thanked her, sitting up to dig in.

"Flaco, heard anything from Less yet?" he asked between bites.

Flaco nodded. "Less is waiting on us. Kev tried calling, but I told him I can only do texts right now."

Weed thought for a moment. "Good. Let Less know to keep it that way. I don't want him saying a word to anyone else until we're done. Need this to go smooth, no slip-ups."

Flaco nodded and got on his phone, sending the message. At this point, all they could do was wait, keep calm, and play it cool. Weed's sister was on standby, the rest of the team was moving into place, and Weed knew the weight of everything rested on this going exactly as planned. He finished his breakfast, took a deep breath, and silently prayed they'd all make it through safely.

CHAPTER TWENTY ONE

Overtime!!

Everyone ate and chilled in the room, passing time until Doc arrived. Weed took another quick nap, stomach full and mind settled from going over the plan a dozen times. When Sexy woke him, telling him Doc was there, he immediately asked Flaco to text Less and check if he could make a move that night.

Doc entered with Pam and Crystal right behind him. Everyone greeted each other, and Crystal sat down next to Weed, grabbing his hand and apologizing again for keeping his daughter, Jazzy, a secret. Weed looked her in the eye and to her to stop apologizing, and to let it go; as long as they made it out of this alive, he was good and grateful for the chance to spend time with his daughter in the future. Crystal nodded with a soft smile. The room fell silent… there was so much to be said but everyone was just in their own zone.

Flaco broke the quiet. "Less says it's a go tonight if we have to, but he warned we'll have to fight for it. They've just put four more guys at the house for the late shift."

Weed quickly calculated. Seven armed men, shit it was gonna be tougher than he thought. He turned to Doc. "You get us fully locked and loaded?"

"Locked and loaded, Weed."

"Good. Let's get ready to move. Flaco, we'll need a G-ride though."

"I got us a Chevy Blazer, all black, at my shop. I have two if we need it."

"No, just the one is all we need. Sexy, do you need your colors on for this?"

"No, Weed, this is your call now."

"Good. Take my bike so you and Crystal can get out of there fast."

Sexy nodded. "I'm on it. Savage just hit me back and said he'll be there!"

"Alright, that gives us time to get into position. Let's move out," Weed said.

Flaco took his bike while Pam, Doc, and Weed got into the truck Doc was riding in, and Sexy and Crystal got on the bike. They followed Flaco to the shop, which was just a short ride away. Once there, Weed told Pam to park out front so they wouldn't have to go back in after finishing the job.

A couple of minutes later, Flaco came out in a black Blazer, wearing black gloves. They all climbed in, careful not to touch anything inside except the door handles. They divided up the AR-15s and 9mms, following Sexy and Crystal to the meeting spot with Savage. At that moment, Weed decided he was going to rely on pure gut and experience for the rest of the night.

When they reached the restaurant, Flaco pointed out the front and back entrances. Weed assigned Doc and Pam to cover the back.

“I’ll take the inside with Sexy and Crystal. Flaco, you cover the front and call me when you see Savage and his crew.”

Doc and Pam took their spots out back and called Weed right away, letting him connect their line with Flaco so everyone would be on the same page. Sexy and Crystal took a table close to the back door, where they could watch both exits without anyone sneaking up on them. Weed settled in a booth nearby.

Doc’s voice came over the line, “We’re set. Pam’s in an old wrecked car, and I’m behind the dumpster. We can see everything. There are cameras covering the back.”

“That’s fine,” Weed replied.

A moment later, Flaco called in, and Weed connected him.

“What’s good, Flaco?”

“The champ is here, but he didn’t come alone. He just pulled up with six of his crew in a Lexus truck. They’re getting out now, right behind me.”

“Got it,” Weed replied. “Doc, you copy that?”

“Loud and clear. Just say the word.”

Weed nodded, feeling the tension heighten. “Is the back still clear?”

“Yep!”

“When you hear me take the first shot at Savage, that’s the signal.”

“Understood.”

"Weed?" Flaco's voice sounded tense.

"Yes, Flaco?"

"Savage is in the front. They're coming in now."

The restaurant layout worked in their favor, with the front entrance and the back exit aligned in a straight line, tables scattered in the center, and booths along the walls. Weed, seated in one of those booths, spotted Savage's face and didn't hesitate. He jumped up and fired two shots, hitting Savage square in the face and head. Savage dropped to the floor instantly.

From the corner of his eye, Weed saw Crystal and Sexy jump up, their pistols drawn, taking shots at the other Deuces. Flaco burst through the front, firing from behind. Doc and Pam came in through the back, shooting with precision. The Deuces didn't stand a chance—they were down before they knew what hit them. Luckily, the restaurant was empty except for them, as three couples had just exited when the chaos began.

Weed turned to Sexy. "Find the manager for me."

Sexy was on it. Meanwhile, Doc cleared the scene of all guns, taking them to the Blazer. Weed, Sexy, and Crystal kept theirs close, just in case.

An older woman approached, and Weed softened his expression to address her properly.

"This is Ms. Smith, the manager," Sexy introduced. "Savage was the owner."

Weed shook his head, quickly shifting back to business. "Ms. Smith, if you can turn a blind eye and take care of any security footage, I'll make it worth your while."

"Forget him," Ms. Smith said, spitting on the floor. "I'll help you, but it's going to cost to let me live and keep my job."

"Not a problem," Weed replied. She shook his hand, led Sexy to the back, and erased all traces of the incident.

Weed heard police sirens approaching, so he hustled to the truck with everything Sexy had gathered. Sexy and Crystal hopped on the bike to follow them to Savage's stash house. Weed's mind raced, wondering why Kev hadn't checked in. He turned to Flaco. "Text Kev and see where he's at." Both men were in the back seat as Flaco gave Pam directions to the house. Kev didn't respond, so Weed asked Flaco to text Less for a status update.

Less texted back as they neared the exit ramp.

"Kev is here now with three other guys, trying to rob us!"

Weed read the message on Flaco's phone. "Tell Less to make his way to the back door and wait until we knock three times. Then he opens up and gets out of the way!"

As they approached the house, Doc handed Weed an AR-15 and an extra clip, then did the same for Flaco. They drove past the house to scope it out. A white utility van sat parked out front, unfamiliar, and everything else seemed quiet. Pam turned down the alley and parked two houses away. They exited the truck and slipped into the backyard, finding Less nervously smoking a cigar.

Less hurried over to Flaco, explaining the situation. "The money's not due to arrive for another twenty minutes. The safes are on timers and only open at certain times, so we've got to get control before the next shipment arrives."

Flaco nodded. Crystal volunteered, "Let Sexy and me go in first. We'll throw them off. You all follow right behind."

Weed agreed. "Alright, but Kev is mine."

Sexy cut in, "No, Weed. If I see him first, he's mine."

Less led them inside through the rear entrance, everyone moving silently. Suddenly, a phone rang. Weed glanced back to see Flaco holding his phone, with Kev's number flashing on the screen. He was in the next room. When the ringing stopped, Weed saw Sexy and Crystal raise their guns and unload on Kev.

Weed swung open the next door, only for a guy from Kev's crew to fire, hitting him in the shoulder. Weed pushed forward, returning fire, hitting the guy with four rounds from the AR-15 before moving to the next room. Each room was barely separated by a door, creating a claustrophobic maze. Less and Flaco appeared, directing them to the basement, where the last two men had supposedly gone.

Flaco noticed Weed's injury. "You good?"

Weed nodded, adrenaline kicking in, knowing that with all the gunfire, nosy neighbors might already have called the cops. They had to secure the safe and whatever else was in the house fast.

They reached a door off the kitchen, where Less signaled them to wait. He knocked in a specific pattern, and the door opened. Just as it did, they heard two shots from upstairs. The basement door started to close again, but Weed fired through it with the AR-15, forcing it open. They descended, spotting a man at the bottom with a fresh wound in his forehead.

Less led them to the stash of drugs and jewelry. Weed looked at Flaco, who was gathering what he could into a large duffle bag. As Weed opened a door off to the side, a woman in a torn wife-beater lunged at him, swinging wildly. He dropped the AR-15 and hit her three times, hard and fast, until she went down. He pulled the sheet off the bed, tossed it to Flaco, and they loaded up the jewelry.

With everything gathered, they moved back to the kitchen, where Doc was at one of the three safes, loading cash into a bag. Right on cue, one of the safes unlocked itself. Just then, the doorbell rang. Sexy and Crystal went to handle it, returning with two men carrying duffle bags. Less took the bags, and Doc and Weed took the men to the basement, tying them up.

The doorbell kept ringing, more men arriving with bags of money. The last group included a man in a leather jacket and slicked-back hair, who Weed assumed was Savage's plug.

Inside, Flaco cut to the chase. "What can we do for you?"

The man replied, "I only deal with Savage. Where is he?"

"He's not here. Again, what can we do for you?"

"I've got one hundred kilos of heroin and one hundred kilos of raw cocaine."

Flaco eyed the bags. "And what do we owe you?"

"1.5 million. Savage told me to come here if he didn't answer."

Weed cut in. "Today's your unlucky day." He glanced at Sexy and Pam, who pulled the trigger on the men holding the bags. Flaco stepped up and shot the man in the head.

In total, they collected twelve bags of cash, two hundred kilos of drugs, and half a bag of jewels. Flaco, Sexy, and Crystal went to the basement to silence the captives, while Weed and Less wiped the security footage.

Once everything was loaded into the truck, Flaco got behind the wheel, and Pam climbed into the back with Weed. They heard Sexy start the bike, and Doc sprinted to the truck.

Pam glanced at Doc. "He must have set the place on fire. Let's go, Flaco!"

Doc jumped in, urging, "Let's roll now!"

As they sped off, they saw the house erupt in flames behind them. Weed slumped back, finally allowing himself a moment to exhale

CHAPTER TWENTY TWO

A Day Late and a Few Million Strong!

Weed was dropped off at the room with Doc and the rest of the crew. Doc looked at Weed, noticing he didn't look too good.

Doc turned to Crystal, "Is there a drug store close by?"

Crystal nodded. "Yeah, we can walk up the street to one."

"Alright, we need to get there now so I can patch up Weed," Doc replied.

After Doc and Crystal left, Pam and Sexy helped Weed out of his shirt, cleaning the blood still oozing from his shoulder, even with Doc's quick bandaging. Despite everything that had gone down, Weed hadn't yet checked his phone to see if his wife or sister had tried to reach him. Knowing he still had business to handle in NYC, he had to stay focused. But first, he needed a quick nap; his eyes were heavy, and he could barely keep them open. Soon, he drifted off.

He didn't know how long he'd been out, but he woke to Doc standing over him, talking on the phone with his wife. Weed's mouth was dry as a desert, and his left side felt immobile. He gestured with his right hand for water. Crystal handed him a cold bottle, and he started gulping it down before Doc stopped him.

“Slow down, my friend. You’re gonna be alright.”

Weed shot Doc a skeptical look but kept drinking slowly. Doc asked if he could talk.

“Yeah,” Weed managed, as Doc handed him his phone. He took it and said, “Hello?”

“James, are you okay, baby?”

“D, I’m fine. Just a scratch. I’ll live.”

“That’s not what Doc told me. He said he took a .40 caliber slug out of your shoulder and you’re stable now.”

“So… it was a flesh wound?”

“James, stop playing with me!”

“Okay, baby. I’m sorry. I’m alright now. How are you?”

“I’m good now. I’ve been blowing up your phone until Doc finally answered. Your sister called too; she’s been trying to reach you and just texted me a second ago.”

“Alright, love. Let me make a few calls and get back to you, okay?”

“James, you’re late getting home. You promised seven days.”

“I know, baby. I’ll make it up to you, I promise.”

“Be careful, Weed. Call me as soon as you’re done talking to your sister.”

“Will do. Love you, D.”

"Love you too, James."

Weed glanced at his watch, realizing he still had a couple of hours to arrange the meet for his sister and Victoria. He called Victoria first; she picked up on the first ring.

"Weed, I was starting to think you weren't coming through."

"Sorry, I got tied up. Can we still do business, Victoria?"

"Absolutely. Just have your people contact me, and I'll give them the time and place to meet. Sound good?"

"Perfect. I'll let them know now."

Weed immediately called his sister.

"Hello, Bro! How are you holding up?"

"I'm okay, sis. I just got off the phone with Victoria. She wants you to call her now to set up the meet. Are you in New York yet?"

"Yes, Bro, we're here and ready. I heard you handled your end?"

"Yeah, it's taken care of."

"Alright, take care of yourself, Bro. We'll handle it from here."

"Got it. You still have her number?"

"Yep, we're good. Later!" She hung up.

Weed set his phone on the nightstand and leaned back, but before he could close his eyes, Sexy asked if she, Pam, and Doc could count the money and split it with Flaco and Less. Weed agreed, and Flaco reminded him they also had the 200 kilos of drugs.

Weed shook his head. "Flaco, like I said from the start, I don't want any part of the drugs. Those days are behind me. I have a daughter now, a wife. I can't take those risks anymore."

Flaco nodded. "Less and I will split the drugs. Just let us take a million dollars each."

Weed looked to Sexy, who nodded her approval. "No problem," Weed replied, then glanced at Less, who looked satisfied.

"Thank you, Weed, and Flaco. This is more than Kev offered me."

"You're welcome, Less. Thanks for staying loyal," Weed replied.

Just then, Weed's phone rang. It was Tiff, so he quickly answered.

"What's good, sis?"

"Change of plans. Stay up until I call you back, alright?"

"Okay. Mind telling me what's going on?"

"We're on the way to meet Victoria now. Just make sure you're up when I call."

"Got it. Love you, sis."

"Love you too. Later!"

Weed sat up in bed to stay alert for the call. Crystal approached, asking if he felt up to talking. He saw the emotion in her eyes and nodded, inviting her to sit beside him. She pulled out her phone.

"Weed, here are some pictures of our daughter." She began showing him pictures, starting from baby photos. His sister was in many of them, even from Jazzy's first day. A mix of joy and jealousy welled up in Weed's chest as he realized he'd missed out on five years of Jazzy's life. He silently vowed never to leave her life again.

Pam and Sexy asked to see the pictures, and Crystal handed her phone to them. While they looked, Weed's phone rang—it was his sister. He put the call on speaker so everyone could listen.

They heard the sound of a car door shutting, then Victoria talking to Tiff, followed by another door slamming shut. Suddenly, two gunshots rang out, followed by two more. Tiff's voice came back on, breathless, "Bro, it's done! We've got the money and the product. Can you call Big Rob to see if he'll take it all?"

Weed just shook his head. Terry took the phone from Tiff, adding, "We're a day late, but we're a couple million richer!"

Weed asked how. She told him there were 100 kilos in the car and $200K in cash in one of the bags.

"Glad you're safe. Now get out of there and meet us in Vegas," Weed said.

"No problem!"

Weed hung up and dialed Big Rob.

"What's up, Weed?"

"My sister's on her way to you again. How much can you buy this time?"

"How much you got?"

"Oh, about 100 kilos."

"What's the price?"

"I'll keep it at $20K a brick, just for you."

"I'll take it all."

"Good. They'll call you when they get there. And they need a legit ride to get to Indy."

"I've got them covered, Weed."

CHAPTER TWENTY THREE

All In a Day's Work!

Weed hit his sister back and let her know that Big Rob would take all the kilos at $20K each.

She replied, "Cool!"

He also told her that Big Rob had a legit car ready for them to get back to Indy.

Both Tiff and Terry chimed in, "Sweet! Good looking out!"

Weed told his sister to call him once she got back to Indy, in case Ms. D wasn't home yet, so she could get into the house, stash the money, and then catch a flight to meet them in Vegas.

"Love you, bro!"

"Love you too, sis!"

Weed tried shifting his position, but the pain was intense. He asked Crystal to turn and face him so he could see her eyes. She did, and he promised her that he'd never leave her or their daughter hanging again. Then he asked her to call Jazzy. Crystal dialed, and as soon as Weed heard his daughter's sweet voice on the phone, his heart melted.

Crystal spoke with Jazzy for a few minutes, explaining who was about to talk to her. Jazzy got very quiet on the other end, then Crystal handed the phone to Weed.

"Hello, Jazzy," he said gently.

There was a pause, and then a shy "Hi."

Weed asked her how she was doing, and she answered that she was fine. Then, out of nowhere, Jazzy asked, "When can I see you?"

Weed looked at the phone and replied, "I'll see you in three days!" She sounded happy and said that would be okay. Weed then asked if she wanted a picture of him before then. She said yes, so he asked Crystal to snap a quick photo and send it over.

At that moment, Doc walked over to Weed and showed him a text on his phone. It was from the Arabs, saying they wanted to buy the other two pieces Doc had shown them and were willing to pay top dollar. Weed nodded to Doc, signaling he was good with the deal.

He talked to his daughter for a few more minutes and got off of the phone, the happiest man on Earth. They laid in the hotel for another two full days. On the last day, like clockwork, he got a call from his wife, telling him that she was at home and everything was put up.

The Arabs had been keeping in close contact with Doc about the jewelry deal. Weed was mostly cool with it, but a nagging feeling told him something was off—especially since they were pressing to wrap things up quickly. Trying to shake off the feeling, Weed got up, showered, and changed into his usual street gear. He wanted to be sure he could handle his bike, so he went outside, started it up, and rode a few laps around the parking lot. Once he felt steady enough, he headed back to the room.

"Weed," Sexy said, phone in hand. "I got the lady from the restaurant on the line."

Weed took the phone and asked where they could meet to talk. She invited him to her home and gave him the address. Weed asked Sexy to jot it down. Flaco overheard and asked if he could tag along, mentioning that he knew the area well. Weed agreed, appreciating the backup. Less, peeking in from the doorway, said he was hungry and wanted to ride too.

They all mounted up and followed Flaco to the address on 74th and Vermont. The neighborhood wasn't bad, though the house could use some work. When they turned off their bikes, the elderly woman approached and invited them in.

Weed instinctively checked for his .45, catching Less doing the same. Inside, her home was clean and tastefully decorated—nothing like the outside. She invited them to sit and offered drinks, which they politely declined.

Weed leaned forward, looking at her earnestly. "Ma'am, I'd like to offer you a partnership in a new restaurant. If you can find a location, I'll buy the building and set you up with everything you need to get started. You'll run it your way, and after the first year, we'll split the profits evenly. I just need to make back a little of the initial investment."

She nodded, clearly excited.

Weed reached into his jacket. "And to help you get started, here's $20,000 to hold you over while we get everything together."

The woman leaped up and hugged Weed so tightly he felt like he might pop! As soon as she let go, he handed her the money. Standing up, he gave her his direct number and told her to call him as soon as she found a building. They all said their goodbyes and mounted up.

As Weed swung his leg over his bike, his phone rang. He fished it out of his pocket and saw it was Big Rob.

"What's up, Big Rob?" Weed answered.

"Man, thanks to you, I'm eating good right now!" Rob replied, sounding pleased.

"Well, Rob, that's cool. So, everything's good?"

"Yep. I was just calling about one of the ladies you sent with your sister—the one that looks like a stripper?"

Weed chuckled. "Lil Bitt? What's up with her? I kind of forgot she went to New York with Terry and my sister."

"Well, one of my boys was trying to get her number, but she took off too fast."

"As soon as I see her, I'll pass that on and hit you back."

"Appreciate it, Weed! And again, good looking out!"

"You're welcome, Rob." Weed hung up, started his bike, and followed the crew. They wanted to grab some food, so he went along. When they stopped, he called Doc to see if he and Pam wanted to join.

"Nah," Doc replied. "Elizabeth hooked us up with a restaurant that delivers."

"Cool. What are you getting?"

"Chinese."

"Order me some too! And what's the update on Vegas?"

"We're scheduled for a sit-down meeting with the head Arab tomorrow evening."

"Alright, sounds good."

After picking up their food to go, they all ate, packed up, and prepped for the highway.

Weed walked over to the motel office and rang the bell. The old man came to the window and asked, "Mr. Tumbleweed, how can I help you?"

"I'd like to settle up on our bill, and thank you for everything."

"Your bill's been covered in full already, Mr. Weed."

"Appreciate it. Can I speak to Elizabeth?"

"Yes, she's been waiting to speak with you. Hold on."

Weed stood there for a moment, and then the office door opened. Elizabeth stepped out, looked around, then pulled him in for a deep, passionate kiss that caught him off guard and left them both breathless. After the kiss, she handed him her cell number and the hotel's contact info.

"Will I ever see you again?" she asked.

"As soon as I get this restaurant paid for out here, I'll be back. Is that cool for now?" Weed said, pulling out a wad of cash.

"Yes, Weed. Just don't take too long, please."

"I won't," he promised. He hugged her and discreetly handed her forty thousand dollars.

"What's this, Weed?"

"It's to hold you over until I'm back this way."

"Thank you!" she said, smiling.

"You're welcome. I'll call you before I come back."

"Okay, Weed. I'll be waiting!"

Doc was walking out of the room as Weed headed back. "Everything good, partner?" Doc asked.

"Yep, I'm ready to hit the highway!" Weed replied, putting what he had into the back of the truck.

Sexy and Pam packed the last of their things while Doc, Flaco, and Less loaded up the truck. Once Weed confirmed he had everything, he tossed his bag in as well and called his sister.

"Hello, brother," Tiff answered.

Weed chuckled. "Tiff, we're getting ready to head out. Do you have a room ready for us?"

"Yep, and a rental truck too. I also got you a bike trailer so you can bring your bike back to Indy."

"Cool. Thanks, sis! By the way, why didn't you mention that Lil Bitt went along with you and Terry?"

"I'll explain when I see you, Bro!"

"Alright, sis. Love you!"

"Love you too, Bro."

"Later!" Weed hung up, waiting as Flaco stored his things in another room, a smart move, considering. Less did the same. With everything set, Weed and his crew said their goodbyes, then hit the highway, bound for Vegas.

The plan was for them to spend two days and one night in Vegas. He was really hoping to keep to this plan, for sure! It took a little longer than he had planned for them to get to Sin City, but as he pulled onto the strip, it felt good to be one step closer to home. They pulled into the parking lot of the Sands Hotel. Doc pulled up next to Weed and said that they had two hours to kill before they met the head Arab.

Weed was still on Midwest time, so he just said, "Ok," and got off of his bike to call his sister.

"What's good, Bro? You in the parking lot yet?"

"Yep, I'm here!"

"You are in room 713. Tell Doc and Pam that they are in 715, right across the hall from you."

Weed agreed and hung up the phone. He headed straight to the elevator to get to the room for a shower. Doc and Pam were right on his heels, with Crystal bringing up the rear. Crystal, Sexy, and I had a room to share and Doc and Pam had their own room. Sis, Lil Bitt, and Terry also shared a room, all on the same floor. Weed entered the room first because Tiff was waiting at the elevator with the keys to their rooms and he got the key first. He hurried to the shower and just wrapped a towel around his waist until he saw his bag on the floor just before he got into the shower. He hurried so the ladies could get their showers. He got dressed real fast because he wanted to get to his sister's room to find out what had taken place in New York.

He hurried to her room and knocked on the door. Lil Bitt opened the door and jumped straight into his arms. "Weed, are you proud of me? I did good. You did not hear a word out of me!"

Weed just smiled at her and told her that he was proud of her and she made him very happy. Then, from the inside of the room, he could hear Terry tell Lil Bitt to let him into the room. Lil Bitt jumped back to the floor and Weed entered the room. He was told to have a seat, so he took a seat at the round table in the middle of the room. Tiff proceeded to let it all roll off of her tongue.

"Bro, we got to Nap, and as you know we had a problem getting the car we needed. Our plug was locked up at the time. From the point when you called Big Rob, everything went uphill. We got the first package from her driver. He was a short, fat, bald man. He looked to be Italian. We took what he gave us and gave him the money. We left him and went to a taco shop and got something to eat on the go. I was hungry, Bro, and I just wolfed the food down. I don't even think I tasted none of it. Then we headed back to Ohio to meet Big Rob once again and he was waiting for us, along with two of his little thugs. One of them kept trying to holler at Lil Bitt, but she did good about not trying to holler back and kept her mouth closed. As we were heading to find a room, I needed to use the bathroom BAD, Bro. I needed to take a shit real bad. I was driving with my cheeks held tight together trying to find an exit off the highway for a rest stop or a gas station. As soon as I saw one, I hurried to the little gas station and rushed to the bathroom. I damn near didn't make it, Bro, for real!"

Weed kept the laugh to himself sot that she could finish telling him what happened.

She continued, "After I went, it started coming out of both ends. I could not even wipe my ass!"

Weed could not hold it any longer and just broke out laughing. So did Terry and Lil Bitt.

"Anyway, Bro, after I got to feeling better, we all put our heads together while counting the money that we got from Rob on how to either let you see us kill Victoria, or at least let you hear. We all agreed that showing this on any public site was stupid, so Terry and Lil Bitt said we should call you and just let you hear. We tried to call your phone and kept trying until finally I called Ms. D and she was also trying to get in touch with you. Finally Doc answered your phone for your wife and in turn, she texted me and said that you had been hit. We got real worried and we were hoping and praying to Jehovah that you were going to be ok! Once we found out that you got hit in the shoulder, Lil Bitt stopped crying. So did Terry. I kept the tears until we really talked on the phone. No after, we headed back to New York. We found out where Victoria was actually living, which was Jessie's old house. It was just a hunch that we followed, but it turned out to be right, so we stayed on top of her and one step ahead of her at all times. We were at the spot to meet her before she was. That's why you only head the car door shut twice and you heard four shots."

"Why is this, sis?"

"When we called you for the meet, we were already there. So was Victoria. She had just met someone else to take care of some other business. That's how we got the money, but I will get to this in a minute. So when we called her, she gave us the spot that she was already sitting at in the backseat of her Lincoln Towncar. She was sipping a drink, while on the phone.

We let Lil Bitt out of the car to sneak up behind the two bodyguards that were in the car with her. We pulled out of the spot we were parked in and went around the corner while we waited for Lil Bitt to get into place. When we saw she was in place, we pulled into the spot in front of her parked car. The reason for this is Victoria knew Lil Bitt, remember?"

"Yes, I do remember, sis. Good thinking! "

"So when I got out of the car, I did not have the money with me because I needed for Victoria to get her lazy ass out of her car! When she did, you could hear Terry and I both put a bullet in Victoria's head. The other two shots were Lil Bitt shutting the two body guards up. Each of them got one bullet to the head. We left her laying in front of her car on the ground and went through the car. We found her money and the drugs. We left one kilo open on the back seat close to her drink."

"I like it, sis! Thank you!"

"It's over now, Bro. Let's get this money divided up and live our lives."

"Ok, I agree, but we have one more thing to contend with and that is the meeting tonight with the Arabs."

"OK, Bro, we got your back, you know this"

"OK, cool. Let's get Doc and Pam so we can have a sit down with these fools." They all left the room together and Tiff kept asking Weed how he got shot. He told her that he would tell her that when she tells him why she kept his daughter a secret from him. The she stopped asking.

They got to Doc's room and he and Pam were both getting ready to leave their room. Doc greeted Weed, "Let's roll, partner!" Weed felt his side and realized he did not have his 45 on his hip. He went across the hall and knocked on the door. Sexy let him in and he went straight over to get his 45 and put it in place on his hip and then left the room. They walked over to the Stardust Casino and went to the high stakes poker table, where Weed saw these fat Arabs in traditional clothing.

As they stood near the high-stakes table, Doc typed a quick message on his phone. Seconds later, he received a reply, and they made their way over to the dining area, settling into a booth. Weed glanced at the menu, his stomach reminding him it had been a long day. Spotting a ribeye dinner special, he flagged down the waiter and placed his order.

Moments later, a large, imposing Arab man approached their table, sliding into the seat across from Weed and Doc. Weed sat back and let Doc lead the conversation, watching as his partner skillfully discussed details unrelated to the deal. He appreciated Doc's careful approach, but his focus sharpened when he realized the man was aiming to buy their entire inventory at a fixed price.

Weed leaned over and tapped Doc's elbow. "Can I chime in for a second?" he asked.

"Of course," Doc replied, giving him the floor.

Weed turned to the Arab man. "If we sell everything to you for one set price, that gives you the power to decide how much you pass along to us. Correct?"

The man nodded, intrigued. "You're not wrong."

"Then let's do this," Weed suggested. "We meet here every six months. We can review what you need and agree on terms for each deal. Fair?"

The man's eyes lit up. "That sounds reasonable. You drive a hard bargain, Mr. Weed."

Weed leaned back, his expression calm. "And as for the jewelry you're interested in—the bracelet and two necklaces from the pictures Doc sent—I believe we agreed on $15 million for the bracelet and $30 million each for the necklaces. That brings us to $75 million, right?"

The Arab man smiled. "Exactly. That is correct, Mr. Weed."

The waiter arrived with Weed's ribeye, and he wasted no time, sliding the plate in front of him with a nod. "Then we've got a deal."

"Doctor, sir," the man turned to Doc, "as always, your payment will be waiting at the cashier's booth across the street, labeled as winnings."

"Perfect. I'll have the jewelry delivered within twenty minutes."

"It was a pleasure meeting you, Mr. Weed," the man said, standing.

"Likewise, Mr. Ahmed," Weed replied.

Once the deal was wrapped up, Doc, Pam, and Terry headed off to finalize the transaction. Back in the hotel room, Tiff and Crystal urged Weed to relax and unwind with them. As they shared stories, mostly laughter and some embarrassing tales from the road, there was a knock at the door.

Weed instinctively reached for his pistol, but Tiff and Crystal, unfazed, walked over to answer it. Weed looked at them like they were crazy.

Weed heard thought he heard Crystal say, "Thank you, Tonya," and he just waited to see what was really going on. That was when this beautiful little girl walked his life. He just stood there with his mouth wide open and he could not move. He felt his throat tighten, his heart pounding in his chest. Weed slowly nodded, hardly able to breathe, and reached down to scoop her up into his arms. She clung to him, and he held her close, feeling his heart burst with joy. He finally managed to whisper, "What's your name, sweetheart?"

"Jazzy," she replied, her voice soft but certain.

He smiled through the tears welling in his eyes. "My name is James."

She giggled and shook her head. "No, it isn't! Your name is Daddy."

Weed's heart melted. In that single, perfect moment, his world shifted entirely. Everything else faded away. He held her tightly, savoring the feeling, silently promising never to let his baby girl go.

Made in the USA
Columbia, SC
02 December 2024

48295054R00074